Fae's Flight

A Fated Fae Novel

For Lizzie
From
LDaye

Luna Daye

ISBN: 978-1-7396888-2-0

Cover by Sarah (Moonrosesxart)
Map by Luna Daye

Fae's Flight

A Fated Fae Novel

Luna Daye

For those who seek adventure,
But who also want to find love, and a place to call home.

Preface:

Please read before starting your adventure. The Fated Fae series is a work of **adult** fantasy fiction. As such it includes mature themes including scenes of a sexual nature, which are described in graphic detail.

A full list of content warnings can be found on my website:
LunaDaye.com

The Humans:

Alana: African/American, black hair, brown eyes, librarian, wears glasses, avid reader- especially fantasy.

Amber: Long golden-brown hair, green eyes, beautician, quiet/secretive.

Riley: Male, ginger, green eyes, history teacher, likes tea.

Edith: Blonde hair, brown eyes, at Uni learning to be a vet, likes star signs, but is afraid of the dark.

Sascha: Black hair, green eyes, vegetarian, creative, animal rights activist.

Willow: Blue hair, grey eyes, free Spirit/hippie, stoner, travel blogger.

Alexis: (Prefers Alex) ginger, brown eyes, community support officer, active/fit, loves music.

Mollie: White blonde curls, blue eyes,

angry/bitter bar/restaurant owner, short.

Charlotte: curvy, honey blonde, green eyes, nerd/gamer, worked in a supermarket, good at strategy (from games)

Yasmin: Deaf, biracial, brown hair, green eyes, loves to paint, and draw.

The Fae

Autumn Court:

Taylen: Mated to Seki, Golden brown hair, chestnut eyes. Water magic.

Seki: Mated to Taylen. Japanese/American, black hair, brown eyes, college drop-out, baker/cake shop owner.

High Lord's brother: Strawberry blonde hair, chestnut eyes. Sight magic, currently imprisoned.

High Lord's half-sister: Dark brown hair, golden brown eyes.

Fae's Flight

Ethea
Winter Court
Autumn Court
Frozen Lake
Summer Court
Spring Court

Chapter 1

High Lord

It is always the same dream. Every night, for as long as I can remember. I close my eyes, and before I know it, I am soaring. Gliding across the sky, heart pounding, wings beating. Free.

The location changes. Usually, I fly over the crystalline waters, glistening shades of aquamarine and sapphire that lap at golden sands in the bay of my beloved Summer Court. My heart sings as I take in the beautifully crafted boats with their colourful sails, the high white cliffs, and the sprawling marble city, encompassed by tall, proud cypress trees. Other times I am greeted with a blanket of green, white, lavender and lemon; the meadows of Spring Court, where the heady aroma of flowers and grass fills the air beckoningly.

Occasionally I soar over the forests of Autumn Court, lush canopies of red, orange and ochre stretching out beneath me and the comforting fragrance of pumpkin and spice. I have even dreamed of gliding over the snow-capped mountains and frozen plains of Winter Court, where the icy wind whips at my skin, the frozen lake glitters amongst the thick snow, and the scent of pine trees fills the thin, cool air.

But it never lasts.

Sometimes the dreams turn nightmarish, and my magic fails mid-flight, my wings vanishing, sending me hurtling to the ground, screaming in terror. But usually, I simply drift back to reality, grounded in my bed.

Today is one of those days.

I rise, dragging the thin cotton sheets away from my clammy skin and make my way to the gauzy curtains that lead out onto the balcony. The marble beneath my feet is comfortingly cool, even though the air is humid. When I step out onto the veranda, the air is heavy. It is thick and muggy, despite it being barely past dawn. *What I would give for a little breeze.*

Below, the pale marble buildings, tainted in pearlescent hues of pink and orange with the rising sun, reach out towards the bay. The turquoise waters sparkle, as if strewn with diamonds.

I grip the low wall, digging my fingers into the warm marble. It doesn't matter that I am naked. This high up in the Summer Palace, no one can see me. As I roll my shoulders, the phantom weight of my wings tugs at my muscles and my body aches to unfurl glorious glistening white feathers. But I mustn't. Tomorrow I am hosting a beach party—as I do once a week—and I will be expected to have my wings on display.

Each time I summon them I feel the drain it has on my magic. I know eventually I won't be able to call upon them at all, and the thought tightens my throat, choking me. Tears sting my eyes as if they were acid, and I clench my fists at my side.

Sometimes I wonder if it wouldn't be worth using the last kernel of my magic in one brilliant burst. I could leap into the sky, soaring high above my court, the air in my lungs, the breeze against my feathers, the sun on my skin. Such a feeling would be worth plunging back to the ground—and my death—for.

A knock at my chamber door drags me from my dark thoughts.

Drawing on a thin robe, I pull open the door to reveal my brother. My twin.

"I hope I did not wake you." It is a statement not a question, but I answer him anyway.

"You did not."

With a curt nod he strides across the threshold, his posture rigid—as it always is—and his ocean blue cape flutters behind him. We are almost identical, he and I, with our cool, dark brown skin and wide set jaws. He is considered by many to be the more handsome brother; despite being the same height, he has a stockier build than I do, broader shoulders and thicker muscles. His stern expression is only exacerbated by his shaved head, and permanent frown, and where my eyes have a decidedly golden yellow tinge to them, his are a colder pale brown that reminds me of seashells.

"Our brother is missing," he informs me, his voice clipped with annoyance.

"He usually is this time of day," I titter.

It is no surprise that our brother cannot be found. He is not fond of the status of being high born, and often shies away from it.

"This is out of character even for him, it has been at least two full days since he was last seen."

"That is unusual," I concede.

My brother huffs out a breath, scratching at the fluff that has begun to grow along his scalp, he is clearly due a haircut soon.

"Send scouts out to his usual locations, he has likely lost track of time. Be sure to send someone to the apothecary. Last time our dear brother disappeared he was found there, working on elixirs to change the colour of hair!"

As I sweep my locs up and twist them in a knot atop

my head, I wonder why he ever needed such a thing. Younger than my twin and I by nearly a decade, I have always tried to shield him from the politics of court, to give him the independence he craves, and allow him to dally as he sees fit. At least one of us should have that freedom.

On his death bed, our father declared that I, instead of my fractionally older twin should succeed him as High Lord of Summer. I have a better head for the running of the court, where my brother, has more of a military mind. I'm the brains, he's the brawn, though neither of us are lacking in either. So, while I run the court, and my twin runs the army, we allow our brother to do as he pleases for the most part.

I did not think it possible, but my brothers face turns even more solemn.

"I sent scouts out yesterday, they searched all the usual places, and everywhere else," his voice changes from irritated to worried.

"Our brother isn't in the city."

Chapter 2

Willow

I should not have had that third blunt.

Hauling myself off my bean bag, legs wobbling slightly, I plod over to the window of my dingy apartment. I glance out into the street below and discover there is hardly anyone about. Strange considering it is late afternoon on Halloween, but then this is a fairly quiet part of town. The part where you won't find any big brand retailers, but lots of little one-of-a-kind shops.

Come Christmas time these streets will be teeming with shoppers looking for unique gifts. Not that I will be here by then. Only one more month and the lease will be up, and I will be free to move on again. Already I feel the tug of wanderlust. Everything has started to feel too familiar, and I *need* a change of scenery. I may even leave the country this time.

I weigh my options; I can either roll another blunt and have a nap, or I can wander to the cute little bakery down the street. My stomach grumbles in answer. Cupcakes it is.

Glancing around the room, blinking to try and clear my foggy vision, I feel a pang woe. The room has no personality. No colour or comfort beyond the basics. It doesn't *feel* like home.

Finally, I manage to locate my bag. It's a bit too large really, but then I do carry a lot around with me. Rummaging inside, I try to locate my keys, then remember I put them in the bowl by the door. I giggle when the keys jangle as I pick them up. Checking my purse is in my bag, I slip on my flip flops.

It's probably too late in the year to be wearing flip-flops, but I hate closed toe shoes, and none of the sensible shoes I own go with the skirt I'm currently wearing: An ankle length patchwork wrap-around, made from tiny squares of sari silk in every colour imaginable. I bought it in a thrift store and it's been my favourite piece of clothing since. I definitely can't pair it with anything but my flip flops.

Leaving my apartment, I float down the stairs. I don't go in lifts when I'm high, they make me feel sick. Although I'm not sure the stairs were a good idea either, as the distance from the bottom keeps changing.

When the floor finally flattens, I plod across the small lobby and push—nope pull— the door open and step out on to the street. A waft of cool, late afternoon air wafts over me and I sigh. It feels nice. It makes my skin all tingly.

Cupcakes.

Refocusing, I look up and down the street, reminding myself which way the bakery is. This way. Turning left I head down the street. I can see the rose-gold sign already and my tummy grumbles again.

Once I am opposite the bakery I pause and check for traffic. This time of day there aren't many cars about, so I should be safe. Just as I am about to cross, the air around me goes…funny. It turns thick and hot and makes me dizzy.

Oh no.

Now is not a good time to throw a whitey. I wonder if I have time to get back to my apartment. Probably not. I close my eyes and take a few deep breaths of the strangely floral smelling air. When I open my eyes again, everything is hazy and…shimmering. As if the air has been filled with glitter. The haze begins to brighten, until all I can see is pure white light.

And then I'm falling. No, not falling, floating. Drifting in the warm comforting light. It's rather relaxing. I think I will stay here a while.

But then it's gone, and I land on my backside with a dizzying thump on damp, mossy earth.

Chapter 3

High Lord

The sun is already low in the sky when I wander down to the beach. Music can be heard all the way back at the palace, and as I join the party, the drums echo in my ears, and my heart beats in rhythm.

A drink is shoved into my hand, and I down it without even thinking, as I amble through the partygoers. All around me people are dancing, drunk and lively. I tuck my wings in tightly, to avoid anyone touching them.

As I make my way to the bonfire, I am met with well wishes and compliments. I simply grin and keep walking, not wishing to engage in conversation.

I know I should try harder, to present a more joyous front, to engage with my people, and at least attempt to enjoy myself. But I cannot seem to summon the strength tonight. I haven't been able to for a while. The weight of the crown is overwhelming—almost unpleasant. Everyone here expects something from me. I wish I could simply enjoy the party as everyone else does, but I cannot.

I am on display. A symbol of the magic that fuels my court, the very essence of fae existence. It chews at my insides that I can feel it fading. Each time I summon my wings I wonder if that will be the last time.

If my magic were to die— and I along with it— rule would fall to my twin. The thought dries my mouth out, as I know he will hate ruling. It is not in his nature. Yet I can feel it sometimes, that bitter wariness he has, as he waits, for my reign to end and his to begin.

I receive another drink, and once again, swiftly pour the sweet liquid down my throat. It only burns for a moment.

Finding a vacant log, I sit beside the bonfire. The vibrant flames twist and coil into the dusk, and I wonder idly if my brother summoned them. I recall when his magic began to manifest, and he struggled to control it. He once set fire to the curtains in our fathers' study, earning him a clout around the back of the head and stable duty for a month. I can't help but chuckle at the memory and find myself searching the crowd for him.

Eventually I find him, sat on a log, across the fire from me, a pretty red head perched on his lap. I watch for a moment as she seductively strokes his chest and whispers something in his ear. My brother—ever the stoic warrior—barely grins at her flirtations.

I roll my eyes and look away.

After downing another drink, I sit quietly and watch the flames dance, and the sky darken overhead. It is a clear night, the crescent moon, and stars clearly visible, and the sight makes my chest ache. What I would give to soar amongst the stars again.

I look back down at the sand, unable to bear the sight of open sky any longer. My eyes follow the patterns in the golden grains until they land on a pair of feet. Glancing up, I find a young fae male stood before me, trepidation contorting his handsome face.

"My Lord, it would be the deepest honour, if you would dance with me."

I simply nod, as I rise from the log, and gesture for him to lead the way. He grins widely, his eyes sparkling in the firelight and heads for the cluster of people next to the drummers.

As we enter the throng, he takes me by the arm and begins a lively dance. Our bare feet stomp and jolt in time with the drums, and for a brief moment, I am lost in the enjoyment of the music and the movement. I think I even smile.

The young fae in my arms is attractive; a slender, toned build, with shoulder length golden curls, and a handsome smile. I can think of worse ways to spend my evening, than dallying with him.

We dance together for two more songs, until the male gets a little more confident, pulling me closer for our third. The drums pound away, as our bodies entwine to the beat. Around us, many have already succumbed to the passion of dancing, and the intoxication of drinks. Beyond the drumming I hear gasps and groans of pleasure, as people rub up against one another, the dances turning more sensual.

As the song comes to an end, my dancing partner times his steps, so they finish right in front of me, with only an inch between our chests. His throat bobs, and his eyes glaze over as he leans towards me. I don't attempt to stop him as his lips brush against mine. Cautiously, he rests his hand against my jaw, rubbing at the stubble he finds there with his thumb. I can taste the wine on his breath.

Though my heart isn't in it, I yield, parting my lips to him, and meeting his kiss stroke for stroke. The young fae's tongue glides along mine, as he leans closer to me, pressing his body against mine so I can feel the outline of his cock. I feel a moment of guilt; mine is nowhere near as hard yet.

Gripping the back of his neck and winding my arm

around his narrow waist I deepen our kiss. His breathing quickens as I explore his mouth with my tongue, and I can feel eyes upon us already.

"Come with me," I command.

Pulling away, I take him by the hand and lead him away from the bonfire. As we make our way around a rocky outcropping to a more secluded spot, the waves lap at our bare feet. I don't speak. What is there to say? His free hand strokes down the outer edge of my wing, and the feathers rustle. The sensation isn't unpleasant, in fact it feels pleasurable, but it is too familiar, too intimate a thing to share with this fae I don't know.

Satisfied we are alone; I turn to face the male. Before I can even catch a breath, his lips are against mine again as he eagerly kisses me. I can't help but smile—it feels good to be desired. I rest my hands on his hips, while his explore me; my chest, my shoulders, my arms, his hands skim over every part of me he can reach. But he does not touch my wings again.

He enthusiastically reaches for the fastening of my skirt, making quick work of the laces and removing the garment swiftly, before dropping to his knees. Without hesitation he grips my hips and runs his tongue up my length. I release a shuddered breath, as my head falls back, and my eyes drift shut. I can't deny how good his hot wet tongue feels against my sensitive skin. He licks up and down, his warm breath teasing, paying extra attention to the prominent vein on the underside. As he twirls the tip of his tongue around my head, I feel myself harden, my pulse quickening.

My hand slides along his shoulder, up his neck to the back of his head as he takes me into his mouth. I release a groan as soft lips glide halfway down my shaft before he pulls back, lightly sucking the tip. Pressing gently on the back of his head, I encourage him to take me again. He obeys, taking me deeper this time and I can't help the roll of my hips.

Relaxing his jaw, he inches further and further down my length until he takes all of me. I enjoy the gagging sound he makes as it echoes off the cliffs that surround us. He pulls away, gasping, sucking in a breath before swallowing me again.

But I don't want to release in his mouth, so I take a step back. Looking up at me from behind thick pale lashes, there is a hint of confusion on his face. He is a handsome male, all tanned skin, and honeyed curls. He is leaner than I am, younger too, and his eyes are pale—in this light I can't quite tell what colour they are, but I imagine them to be blue, like the sky on a clear midsummer's day.

I take his chin between my thumb and pointer finger. "Stand."

He obeys again, and I admire his glistening swollen lips. Without a word I reach between us and unfasten his skirt. It falls to the ground with a rustle, revealing his proud hard cock and I feel the faintest stirring of lust. The male before me pants, his chest heaving, and I notice the head of his cock is already beading with moisture—it won't take him long.

Good.

When I reach down and palm him, he releases a ragged sigh, fingers digging into my shoulders. I wrap my fist around him, pumping only thrice before pulling away my hand and walking around behind him.

"Against the rock," I command, my voice thicker than it was before.

The blond male takes a few steps forward, resting his forearms against the stone, bracing himself. As I step up behind him, I nudge his feet further apart, so he is the right height, and he arches his back, presenting himself to me.

I can't help but skim a hand over the soft roundness

of his ass, then glide up his hip as I step closer to him. Spitting on my hand, I rub it against the head of my cock. I hear him suck on his fingers before he reaches around to lubricate himself. Once he is satisfied that he is wet enough for me, he returns to his arched position against the rocks. Taking my cock in hand, I rub myself up and down the crease of his back side, as he hums with anticipation. I line myself up to him, and ease in gently, eliciting a gasp from the handsome male. One hand holds his hip, and with my free hand I caress his spine as I press deeper.

"Yes," he groans as I fill him.

He leans into me, his backside now flush against my hips, and I can't deny it feels good to be inside him. I pull back slowly, withdrawing from him inch by inch. When only my tip remains, I pull on his hips and ease back into him, eliciting another groan. He is looser now, and it is easier for me slide in and out of him.

Gripping his hips tightly I quicken the pace, thrusting into him, enjoying the sound of our skin slapping. The blonde fae is panting as I grind into him, and I know he is already close. Sliding my hand along his clammy skin, I reach around his body, taking his firm length in my fist. When he gasps with pleasure, I tighten my grip and begin to pump him in time with my thrusts. His body bucks and jolts against mine.

"Yes! My lord!" He cries, as his muscles clench around me.

He shudders in my hand, and I hear his spend splatter the sand. His release pulses through him, sending his muscles rippling and with a grunt I find my own. It is quick and weak, but I find it, nonetheless.

I withdraw, as shame and disappointment begin to war inside me. I feel nothing for this fae, no emotional connection whatsoever. Physical attraction and pleasure are one thing, but it always leaves me feeling lacking…

incomplete somehow.

Wandering over to a rock pool, I splash my cock with the cold salty water, wincing as I clean myself off. The mild discomfort feels almost fitting. When I stand and turn, I find the young fae leaning with his back against the rocks, a satisfied grin across his handsome face. Reaching down, I gather our clothing, shaking them free of sand, and hand his to him.

"Thank you, My Lord."

His voice is dripping with gratitude as he takes his skirt and knots it around his lean waist. I can only summon a weak smile, as I re-dress. All I want now is to be alone.

"Leave me," I command.

Disappointment dances across the young fae's face but he nods and obeys. The moment he disappears behind the outcropping I draw in my wings, the soft fluttering sound they make as they vanish claws at my chest.

I decide not to return to the party, knowing I will be unable to enjoy myself, or even pretend to. Instead, I walk the long way back, avoiding the crowds on the beach, and walking down the quiet back alleys of the all but deserted city.

Melancholy follows me like a shadow back to the palace. How long has it been since I last genuinely enjoyed a tryst? I have had plenty of them, male and female both. But when did I last feel anything more than fleeting lust for anyone?

It's been years.

I know what I want, even though I will never have it. Such a thing has not occurred in Ethea for decades, a century even. I long for that one person with whom I can share everything, whose existence has been bound to my own by the Fates. A partner, lover, friend… a blessing. I long for a mate.

Chapter 4

Willow

Dew still glitters on the lawn, and mist clings to the trees as I sit on a bench in the garden of Autumn Court. I have made a habit of getting up early and strolling through the grounds since I arrived here three days ago.

Yesterday I managed to score some herbs from the High Lord—well his gardener—so todays morning walk had even more purpose; to find a pretty spot to sit, smoke and relax. I don't see the point in stressing out about being here. I may as well enjoy myself.

As I breathe out, the cool morning air billows in front of my mouth and I smile at the smoke shapes. Ahead, the pumpkin patches dapple the grounds with bright orange orbs and swirls of vibrant green. Beyond them, the Autumn Court Palace reaches up into the golden dawn overhead with spires of poppy red.

As I take another drag from my pipe and wiggle my toes in the cool damp grass, I grin cheerfully, as I imagine myself to be in the pages of a fairy-tale book.

I close my eyes and listen to the birdsong in the trees and the gentle rustle of leaves as the wind blows through them and tickles my skin. As I breathe deep, the fresh morning air intense in my lungs, I catch the already familiar scent of breakfast wafting from the palace.

Time to join the others.

Standing, I tuck my now empty pipe back into my bag, next to my little pouch of herbs, alongside my journal and other belongings. I've lived out of a bag before, but that was more of a rucksack. I literally had fifteen items on me when I was sucked through a magic portal, which is more than any of the others. Most of the other humans that arrived when I did, had nothing more than the clothes on their backs.

As I make my way the palace, the bright orange dress—which Alex refused to wear when the High Lord gifted it to her—sways around my ankles and makes a pleasing swishing sound.

I pass through the huge stained-glass wall, a kaleidoscope of colours dancing in the morning sun, and head through the lobby to the banquet hall.

As always, a spread of just about every breakfast food imaginable has been laid out. There are platters of fruit, little bread rolls with butter and jam, mini pastries and tarts, sausages, and eggs, even some weird little oat cookies that have been glazed with honey. Unusually, I am the last to arrive.

"Willow!" Charlotte calls me over, gesturing to the seat to her left.

"Morning gorgeous," I greet as I plonk down beside her with a swish and a jangle.

I'm pleased to see she has left her hoodie back in her room, and instead is draped in maroon silk.

"Now, that you are all here," The High Lord begins, "I have made arrangements for half of you to go and stay in Summer Court."

"Ooo that sounds like fun!" I squeal, remembering the map Alana found in the library. The Summer Court sits on the coast—I love the beach…

Apparently, I am the only one excited about the

announcement, as everyone else is getting angry or upset about it and talking over one another.

"I know you have a lot of concerns," the High Lord states calmly. "I assure you; you will be well taken care of by the High Lord of Summer Court. It is a pleasant place. I'm sure those of you who choose to go will enjoy your stay there."

Another round of angry questions ensues, all of which he answers. Explaining that it is only temporary, because of a resource problem, and that we can decide amongst ourselves who will go.

I get an excited flutter in my tummy, when he tells everyone, that those who go will travel by horse, and that it will take three days to get there. I love horse riding!

"How long must we stay there?" Mollie demands.

"Is the way dangerous?" Charlotte asks.

The High Lord rubs his short beard, looking stressed. I'm not surprised.

"The road has… some slight dangers, but nothing my guards cannot handle. I assure you; you will be safe. And as for how long… I don't know. As long as it takes to summon enough magic to cleave open another portal. But you have my word, that you will be called upon, and returned here when the time comes."

The others discuss pros and cons for a while, but no one puts themselves forward…

"Well. I'm happy to go," I announce, leaning back in my chair.

"Me too," adds Edith.

Sascha then coaxes Mollie into going, promising that it will be like a beach holiday. Mollie only agrees, after she has made several demands of the High Lord. I'm sure he will be glad to see the back of her.

That's four of us… The High Lord is probably hoping that at least five of us leave for Summer Court.

Charlotte glances at me, her bottle green eyes uncertain. After I give her a smile and an encouraging nod, she agrees to go too, completing our group.

"Very well, I will make arrangements, be ready to depart at midday."

As the High Lord strides from the room, leaving everyone to discuss Summer Court, I scarf down some breakfast, eager to return to my room. I mentally make a list of everything I need to do before we depart. I want to make sure I don't leave any of my things behind, and that my journal is up to date. I was going to hunt down some fallen autumn leaves, to add a bit of colour to the pages—not that I have any glue…

I also wonder if I will have time to have another quick smoke before we set off.

Chapter 5

High Lord

I bristle when I see the iron clamped around my brother's wrists. He's been stupid, no doubt, but the magic dampening metal seems excessive. The Autumn Court guards keep a cautious distance from him as they escort him towards me, the thud of their boots echoing off the marble throne room floor. My brother's warm, dark skin looks ashen, and has blistered around his wrists. While his usually vibrant brown eyes are sunken and dull, and he wears a pained expression on his face. I clench my jaw, considering that he has been marched through the city in this condition—like a criminal.

The Autumn Court guards halt several feet from me, and when my brother stops with them, he wobbles in place. He is weak.

Have they had him in iron the entire journey back?

Relieved that I arranged to receive my brother in private, rather than in public, I rise from my seat, keen to have this nasty business over with.

"I'm sure you are weary from your travels. I have arranged rooms for you, which my brother will escort you to, and when you are rested, you shall feast."

I gesture to my twin, who stands stoically to one side.

His expression does not shift as he nods and turns, leaving the throne room. The Autumn Court guards follow him, and I am left alone with my younger brother. When the door slams shut, he falls to his knees with a sigh, head bowed. I rush across the distance between us, ignoring the heavy, uncomfortable weight of the iron in the air, and kneel in front of him.

He looks up at me through thick, damp lashes, as tears roll down his cheeks.

"I didn't mean… I didn't—" he chokes.

"Here," I reach for his cuffs, wincing as the harsh metal stings the skin on my fingertips, and pull the pins that hold the cuffs in place.

When the awful restraints clatter to the floor my brother doubles over with a groan and empties his guts, splattering the marble beside us. He sucks in a breath and slumps back on his heels looking pitiful.

"Come on, let's get you cleaned up," I tell him as I rise from the floor.

He takes my outstretched hand and staggers to his feet, swaying unsteadily. I pull his arm over my shoulders and wrap an arm around his waist to lead him back to his chambers. I also make a mental note to send house staff to clean up the throne room.

My brother leans on me as we traverse the white marble halls of the Summer Palace. The song of sea birds and sounds from the harbour drift in through open windows, where colourful gossamer sways in the breeze. As the sheer fabric parts, I spot perfect cloudless skies and the glittering waters of high tide. My heart clenches in my chest with the desire to soar above it, and marvel at the beauty of my court. But now is not the time for my own melancholy.

Once back in his chambers, my brother slumps onto the edge of his bed. Fortunately, I had the foresight to acquire some remedies from the palace healer beforehand and pull over a small table laden with jars and bottles.

"Here," I instruct, kneeling at my brother's feet and handing him a tonic to help alleviate his iron sickness.

He gulps it down with a screwed-up face, then thanks me. I have just finished anointing a cloth with a healing balm when my twin storms through the door. He strides across the room and clouts our younger brother round the back of the head. "You fool! You had us worried sick!"

"Brother," I rebuke, "At least wait until his sickness has worn off before you begin your chiding."

My twin nods, a frown knitting together his dark brows. He grumbles as he too sits on the bed, taking our brothers hand and examines one blistered wrist. "Those iron shackles were completely unnecessary," he huffs.

"I agree," I say, as I take our brother's other wrist. "Tell us what happened," I encourage gently, as I start to dress the branded skin.

"I assumed you already knew."

"The High Lord of Autumn sent an explanation, but I would hear your version of events."

Wincing as I dab his swollen skin, my brother takes a deep breath before responding. "I received a letter from the Autumn Lord, he said he'd been having visions of his mate, that he'd *seen* her. When he discovered that she's human, he understood that the only way to meet her and claim her was to bring her here. It sounded almost too good to be true. A mate for one of the high fae, after all this time…"

He winces again as I clean a particularly unpleasant wound, while my twin looks on with irritated interest.

"He said that with my illusion magic, and his visions, we could pinpoint a portal that would find her, and pull her through to our realm."

My twin scoffs. "Pulling a human through a portal,

against their will—utter foolishness."

I glare at him, then nod to our brother, encouraging him to continue.

"He explained that it would work best on Samhain when the veil is thinnest. He sounded so…desperate."

"You should have told us, before you left Summer Court." I tell him gently.

"You would have tried to stop me."

"Of course, we would have!" My twin shouts as he rises from the bed and begins pacing. His frustration is plain in the tension he holds across his shoulders and the scowl on his face.

"I assume you already know that the portal was more powerful than either of you anticipated, and you actually pulled through eleven humans." I explain to our younger brother, who's eyes have not lifted from the floor since he sat on his bed.

He nods with a sniff, his bottom lip trembling. "Forgive me brother," he sobs. "I only wished to help."

"I know," I comfort. "You have a gentle heart. It is not in your nature to refuse your friends, even when you *should.*"

The High Lord of Autumn *assured* me that his own brother was being punished for the cleaving, but I don't have it in me to do the same. Despite being only ten years younger than myself I always perceive the young man before me as my *little* brother. I will always seek to protect him. Perhaps that makes me weak, but as I behold him, skin blistered and swollen, eyes sunken and dull, looking utterly miserable, any thoughts I may have had of punishment desert me. He has suffered enough.

I wrap some soft gauze around my brother's wrists before continuing.

"I should inform you that as a result of your… involvement in the cleaving, we have been asked to play host to some of the humans."

When my twins' gaze jolts to mine I meet it squarely.
"You didn't tell me that," he hisses "I hope to the fates you refused. Just because our brother was roped into opening the portal, doesn't make the humans our responsibility—"

"I have agreed." I earn a scowl from one brother and a look of confusion from the other. I knew my twin would disapprove, so I sent the reply yesterday without telling him.

"The High Lord of Autumn is sending five of them here. They are likely already on their way."

Chapter 6

Willow

"It will take us a month to reach Summer Court at this rate!" The Autumn Lady huffs as Charlotte hops down from her horse and rushes into the woods.

Edith and I giggle. It's *only* the fourth time today we have stopped so someone could pee.

"Why is she so grumpy?" Edith whispers.

"No idea," I shrug.

"How much further *is* it?" Mollie demands, receiving an eye roll from our guide.

"Speaking of grumpy," I murmur, earning another snicker from the giggly woman beside me.

"The border is just beyond that rise and marks the halfway point."

Mollie mumbles something to Sascha, and the two grumble. The small blonde has been moaning the entire journey: her saddle is uncomfortable, she doesn't like the food, her butt is sore, she never wanted to travel to Summer Court anyway, are we there yet? It's kind of bumming me out.

Leaning forward, I stroke the flanks of the horse I'm sat atop. None of the guards seemed to know his name, so I gave him one myself.

"You're such a good boy, Pumpkin," I coo as I rub the side of his neck, to which he snorts.

"I can't believe you called him Pumpkin," Charlotte remarks as she emerges from the woods.

"It's the perfect name for him," I insist. "He came from Autumn Court, and he is the most gorgeous ginger boy. Aren't you Pumpkin? Yes, you are!"

He snorts again as Charlotte hoists herself back up into her own saddle and we embark once again.

For two days now we have ridden through a sprawling forest, which, according to the map Alana found, covers most of the Autumn Court. As far as I can see there is stunning woodland, a vibrant landscape filled with reds, oranges, and golds. Behind us is a range of snow-capped peaks in the distance, far to the north. It reminds me of the time I travelled to Canada and spent time in the Laurentian Mountains.

Alana also explained that Ethea *does* have seasons, and that even though the weather doesn't change much, each court's magic is strongest during their own season.

The temperature seems to rise with each mile we venture further south, and I'm glad I opted for the clothing I crossed into Ethea in. My faithful patchwork skirt, which is wonderfully comfortable and breezy, and a sky-blue vest top. I don't know how Sascha is coping in all black, or Charlotte…

"Aren't you hot in that hoodie?" I ask her.

She flushes and looks down at the thick grey garment. "No," she insists, but I hear the lie.

I wish she had the confidence to show more skin. She's the fullest figured amongst us, and she's absolutely gorgeous. It makes me sad that she doesn't see it. When Edith catches my eye, we exchange a look that tells me she agrees. I make a silent vow to try and give her confidence a boost while we are on this adventure together.

I direct Pumpkin down the dirt track confidently, as Edith and Charlotte strike up a conversation about video games. I have nothing to contribute, having never played one, but I'm content to sit and listen to the pleasant sound of their chatter.

Sascha and Mollie talk quietly ahead of us and whatever they are discussing, it seems to have Mollie riled up…again. I can tell from the tone of her voice, even if I cannot hear her words, that she is irritated by something and do my best to ignore it.

Further ahead, the Lady of Autumn Court leads us silently, flanked by four guards, while the other eight follow behind us. I find their presence a little unnerving—they're all so uptight—but I suppose it is necessary to make sure we get to Summer Court safely.

By mid-afternoon, the trees start to thin, their colouring shifting from the vibrant fiery hues of autumn to bright lush greens. Eventually woodland gives way to fields that roll out in every direction. I can see groves and orchards, as well as pastureland with the occasional spattering of livestock—we must be getting close to the court itself.

Without the canopy of trees, the sun shines down on us, pleasantly warming my skin. I look up at the expanse of bright blue sky overhead, catching sight of a murmuration of birds and can't help the grin that tugs at my cheeks. The heat, however, becomes a challenge for the others, and Mollie takes up her favourite activity. Complaining. Sascha joins in but not as vehemently, it is as if she is only doing it to pass the time.

I smile with satisfaction when Charlotte finally concedes and removes her hoodie. She bites her lip and looks down at herself in the slightly less baggy t-shirt and with a sigh, ties her hoodie around her waist.

Her conversation with Edith shifts to a film franchise I'm not familiar with, so once again I amble beside them in content silence, glad they seem to be enjoying themselves. Their conversations are much more pleasant than the ones I imagine Mollie and Sascha to be having. I appreciate their company quietly, comfortable not really joining in as I am too distracted by the beautiful landscape surrounding us.

By the time the sun begins its descent, my butt is so sore I consider jumping off Pumpkin and walking for a while, but I have worn my flip-flops, so walking probably isn't the best plan—

"We stop here for the night," the Lady of Autumn Court informs us, and I sigh with relief.

In a flurry of activity, the guards dismount and set up camp. They work silently and efficiently, and it isn't long before they have pitched a handful of small tents, with a campfire in the middle. Edith and Sascha insist on helping care for the horses, while I sit between Mollie and Charlotte. I pull my pipe from my bag and start packing it with herbs. When I light it, I momentarily wonder what I will do when my lighter runs out.

"Ugh, not again. Don't you have anything different?" Mollie moans, when the travel rations are divvied up. I notice that her usually tight, platinum blonde curls have started to turn fuzzy in the rising humidity. Her head looks a bit like a cloud.

We are given the same food as we have been the last two nights. An apple or pear, a thick slice of sweet pumpkin bread and a few strips of dried meat which Sascha refuses to eat because she is vegetarian.

"Here, wash it down with some of this," Sascha encourages, handing Mollie a bottle of something, wine I assume.

The bottle is passed around, but when it reaches me, I decline. "I'm good, thanks," I explain raising my pipe, lighting it, and taking another drag. I instantly relax. The heady smoke soothes my aching muscles and sets my head tingling.

These herbs are strong.

Adequately chilled, I tuck into the food, grateful that it has been provided. The juice from the pear tingles along my tongue, causing me to hum in appreciation. The meat strips—which remind me of jerky—are wonderfully salty, but make me thirsty, and I slurp down probably more than my fair share from the water skin that is handed around. I save the pumpkin bread for last because it's my favourite. Heavy, slightly spicy, and heavenly sweet, it tastes like a hug, and I can't help but smile while I eat it.

"I take my leave," the Autumn Lady informs us—I wish I knew her name. "We are in Summer Court territory now humans, make sure you seal your tents to protect against scorpions."

"Scorpions?!" Edith shrieks.

She is ignored, as our guide rises from her seat with an irritated sigh and disappears into her tent.

"She's kidding right?" Charlotte asks.

"I doubt it," I say with a grimace. "The terrain here reminds me of when I was backpacking around southern Australia, and they had tonnes of scorpions, especially at night when it cooled down."

"This is ridiculous," Mollie moans, "Surely there is a hotel, or at least an inn or something between the two courts?"

"Apparently not," Sascha chips in, before the two of them start yet another complaint fuelled conversation.

"Well, I'm going to call it a night," I announce after taking a final drag from my pipe and tipping the ash out on the ground beside me.

"Night," they all bid me when I stand from the log I have been perched on and make my way to one of the smaller single-man tents.

There are some larger two-man tents, but *apparently,*

I snore, so none of the others want to share with me, but I don't mind. I'm quite content in my own little snug den. Quickly checking the inside for creepy-crawlies, I peel back the bed roll, then once satisfied I'm not going to be a bug snack, I seal myself in.

Nestling down into the bedding, on top of the sheets—because it's too hot to sleep under them, I close my eyes and listen to the campfire crackling and the soft hum of conversation beyond the canvas walls.

In the distance I can hear what sounds like cicadas chirping, and for a moment I'm sure I can hear the far-off roar of the ocean. It's been a while since I last saw the sea, longer still since I last swam in it. An excited shiver dances over my skin, as I try to imagine what adventures await at Summer Court. Giddy anticipation wars with the calming effect of the herbs until, eventually, I drift off into a peaceful, dreamless sleep.

Chapter 7

High Lord

A crowd has gathered to greet the humans to Summer Court. I know neither myself nor my twin told anyone of their arrival, so I assume it was our younger brother. The energy in the city pulses, as the people anticipate seeing *the humans.*

It is not far from dusk when the caravan appears at the city gates. I grip the balcony railing and watch as the visitors head down the wide straight road that leads directly to the Summer Palace. The street is lined with curious citizens, and I wonder what the humans think of the welcome.

At the front of the procession is the Lady of Autumn Court, behind her are four guards, then the five human females, then another eight Autumn Court guards.

I sigh as I pull away from the balcony and head down to the throne room. The pressure of being responsible for an additional eighteen people sets my pulse quickening. I will be able to send some of the guard's home, but if the Lady of Autumn decides to stay for a while, so will her guards, on top of the five humans… I hope the High Lord of Autumn has a plan to send them home soon, as I am unsure how long I will be able to provide for them all.

The slap of my sandals on marble echoes off the walls as I pace through the palace. I turn the last corner and find my twin stood rigidly by the throne room door, awaiting my arrival.

"Brother," he nods.

"Brother."

"I will say it one last time. I do not think this is a good idea—"

"I know." He has told me several time already. "But as our brother had a hand in dragging them here, it is only right we help shoulder the burden."

"Our brother was *coerced*, it was the Autumn Lord's idea."

"And yet if our brother hadn't participated in the cleaving, the humans would not have arrived in Ethea in the first place."

I push through the throne room doors and head for the raised dais.

"Then I hope the High Lord of Autumn finds a way to return them to their own realm promptly," my brother adds, echoing my earlier thoughts.

"As do I, though I doubt it will be as promptly as we would like. In his letter, he told me that he had imprisoned his own brother for what was done. The Autumn Lord's magic will not replenish while he is in iron, so I fear the humans will be our responsibility for some time."

My twin scoffs as I lower myself onto the throne and he stands sullenly beside me.

"I assume my instructions have been carried out."

"Yes," my twin answers, as our brother enters and comes to stand the other side of me, delight plain on his face. He does not understand the gravity of the human's arrival here, and I haven't the heart to spoil his excitement. "Rooms have been made available, a feast planned for this evening—not that we have the means to keep feasting like this—and appropriate Summer Court clothing has been provided."

"Thank you."

My twin merely grunts.

In anticipation for the throne room doors opening, I sigh and roll my shoulders, summoning my wings. I try not to wince as shimmering white feathers unfurl and I feel the harsh abrasion of my magic draining. My throne has been carved to accommodate the huge wingspan, and with a rustle I settle them into place. The weight of them both a comfort and source of anguish.

How much longer will I be able to summon them?

Before I can tumble into self-pity the main doors burst open, and my visitors enter the throne room. Horses stabled; the Lady of Autumn now leads the group across the pale marble on foot. Her warm brown skin gleams as she glides towards me, her floaty, copper dress billowing behind her—hardly appropriate travel attire. Behind her the five human females shuffle along, gaping at the grand marble room they have entered.

"Welcome," I greet, trying to keep my voice courteous.

One of the humans, much shorter than the others, with white, blonde hair glares at me, as if somehow unhappy to be in my court. The one beside her dressed all in black doesn't look best pleased either. I try not to take offence. I do not know what kind of surroundings the humans are accustomed to.

Another two blondes walk in the middle of the group, one of which is much fuller figured than the rest. They at least look happy to be here, but it is the one on the right that catches my attention.

This human jangles as she walks, and I notice that the sound is coming from metal hoops decorating her wrists. Her hair is the same azure blue as the waters in the bay and cascades down her back like waves, complimenting her skin, the colour of which reminds me of wet sand. Even though she is pale skinned, she if beautifully tanned and clearly spends a lot of time outside. I am mesmerised as she peers around the room with nothing short of awe on her face. When her gaze falls on me, and silvery-grey eyes meet mine, my chest seizes, and my breath catches in my lungs. I attempt to stop the panicked rustle of my wings and fail, as I stand, yielding to the undeniable tug I feel towards this woman.

My mate.

"Brother," my twin hisses beside me.

"Right," I mutter, my hospitality utterly forgotten. "Welcome to Summer Court. Rooms have been made available for you, and tonight, a feast will be held to celebrate your arrival."

The humans mutter amongst themselves as the Lady of Autumn approaches me. It is a little too familiar to ascend the dais steps to my throne, but the haughty expression on her face tells me she doesn't care.

"High Lord," she bobs her head.

"Lady."

"I am weary from travel and keen for some *fae* company, please escort me to my room," she demands.

I am torn. I should do as she has asked, even if it is not her place to make such demands. It is the hospitable thing to do. Yet, right there, twenty feet away stands my mate. I try to catch her attention again, but she is once more gazing around the room, eyes glittering, mouth slightly agape in admiration.

"Of course," I answer grudgingly. The humans are staying for a while, I will have plenty of time to acquaint myself with my mate.

The Lady of Autumn links her arm through mine, an appreciative smile on her face, and before I even realise I have done it, I lead her from the room, down the corridor and towards the guest wing.

She is talking to me. I can hear the scratchy hum of her voice beside me, but I don't discern any words. It's like having my head underwater, the sounds are muffled and far away. All I can think about is *her.* The blue haired female I have just walked away from. Already I feel the tug of our bond, beckoning me to return to her and it takes all of my strength not to turn and race back to the throne room.

I hasten my steps, eager to deliver the Lady of Autumn to her rooms, so that I might seek out the human woman who jangles as she walks. My mate. *Fates*. I have a mate.

This changes everything.

Chapter 8

Willow

Summer Court is more beautiful than I could have imagined. Autumn court was pretty, sure, but Summer Court is…*wow.*

Standing on the balcony attached to my guest room, I look out over the sprawling marble city below. Turquoise tiled roofs, and colourful flags break up the pristine white of the buildings. Beyond, vast wooden verandas reach out over shimmering aquamarine water that glitters even in the weak rays of the setting sun. If it looks this beautiful at dusk, I can't even imagine how amazing it will look in full daylight.

Already my feet itch to go exploring, to wander and see all that Summer Court has to offer, but I should probably join the others for our feast tonight. There will be plenty of time for adventure tomorrow. I bounce up and down on my toes, giddy with excitement.

A knock at my door pulls me back into the main room. "Willow?" Charlotte calls through pale wood.

"In here," I confirm.

When she enters my room, she is clutching a bundle of fabric, and her eyes look red and puffy.

"This is a nightmare!" She cries, a sob breaking from

her throat. "It's Autumn Court all over again. Are there seriously no plus sized fae!" She sniffs, launching the fabric from her hands onto my bed.

"Oh, Char," I soothe. "We can work something out, let me see those." I reach for the garments she has already discarded and hold them up.

"Here, see this one is a wrap around," I tell her, holding up a floaty cream dress.

"I tried that one, it won't reach around my tummy." Her bottom lip wobbles as she plonks herself down on my bed.

"Hmmm, I'm sure we can figure something out, we did at Autumn Court, right?"

The second day after we arrived in Ethea, the High Lord of Autumn presented us all with new dresses. Donated by his sister apparently. Unfortunately, he didn't consider Charlotte's fuller figure. While we were all downstairs enjoying dinner, I noticed she was missing and when we returned to our rooms, I checked on her, only to find her crying because she was the only one without a new dress to wear, as the one given to her didn't fit.

Well, I wasn't having that. Luckily, I'm a dab hand with a needle and thread. So, I asked around to find a more flowy dress, and managed to make some minor alterations so that it fit her. And the gowns maroon colour was gorgeous against her pale skin and honey blonde hair.

I consider the garments I have been gifted and find that I have a wrap around too, in a pale seafoam green.

"I have an idea," I announce, "look, I have a wrap around one too, why not try them both on at the same time?"

"Huh?" Charlotte wrinkles her nose at me, not seeing my vision.

"Here." When she stands, I fold hers over, and drape

one garment over her left shoulder, then do the same with mine, and drape it over her right. Spinning her around, I manipulate the fabric so that the two sides meet at the base of her back, and fabric falls gracefully over her curvy bum, then turn her back around to face me.

I pull the two side over her boobs, creating a gorgeous vee of cleavage, and hold the edges to the side of her waist.

"Now all we need to do is add a few stitches and voila! Two-tone wrap around," I beam at her.

She replaces my hands on her hips, holding the garment ends in place and wanders over to a floor length mirror on the far wall. Tilting her head, she assesses my creation then gives a little twirl, the cream and seafoam fabric fluttering about her generous curves.

When she turns back to me, she is grinning.

"I like it!"

"You look gorgeous, Char."

She all but skips back over to me and stands before me so that I can stitch the newly formed dress into place.

Pulling the mini sewing kit from my bag, I select the white thread and, licking the end, thread my needle.

"So, the High Lord is pretty dreamy," Char admits.

I chuckle. "I suppose he is."

"He has wings. None of the other fae I have seen have *wings!*"

"I didn't really pay him much attention. The throne room was stunning, even if it was weirdly hot in there."

"Hot? I thought the room was a bit chilly."

"Really?"

"Yeah."

"Huh, I felt all weird and tingly," I shrug, biting the end of the thread, and starting again on another patch of fabric. Maybe I smoked too much this morning, but it was definitely hot in the throne room. My chest was practically vibrating, and I could feel my cheeks flushing.

"I'm going to go and explore the city tomorrow, want to come with me?" I ask. I will be content either way; I'm used to spending time on my own, often travelling alone, as I've been fending for myself since I was seventeen, but I enjoy Charlotte's company.

"Sure," she grins.

I have barely finished sewing up all the loose edges of Charlotte's dress when there comes another knock on my door. Expecting it to be one of the others, I jump up from my kneeling position on the floor to open it.

A servant of some kind is stood beyond the threshold. "The feast is ready for you, if you would follow me, please."

I turn to Charlotte who grins and follows me as I let the servant lead us down the corridor. The dark skinned fae weaves silently along the corridors, nodding their head to the other servants bustling about their business as we pass. Their hair is pulled back in a neat bun and I notice that her ears are not as pointed as the high fae's.

It isn't long until we enter a hall with a long wooden table. The room is decadent, thick white columns support a high ceiling, and open windows draped in sheer fabric let in the last of the days light. High three-pronged candelabra, like tridents, hold candles which illuminate the feast on the table before us.

The spread makes my mouth water. Trays of salad and bowls of olives, cubes of seasoned meats and cheeses, small flaky pastries, and flat breads beside bottles of oil infused with what looks like chillies and garlic.

Chatter behind us alerts me to the others' arrival, and we take our seats. Sascha grins at the food laid out, most of which is vegetarian friendly, and for once Mollie doesn't complain, eagerly filling her plate. Summer

Court cuisine must be more to her taste.

"Welcome," greets a dark skinned fae male as he enters the room. I recognise him from the throne room. He was stood to the left of the High Lord, with a youthful face, bright warm brown eyes, and a rather impressive head of tight coils.

He is quickly joined by another fae, one who looks astonishingly similar to the High Lord—his twin I assume. Yet where the High Lord had long locs, this fae has his hair shaved short, and instead of seeming welcoming as the High Lord had, he wears a scowl. He also doesn't have wings.

They sit either side of the slightly more elaborate chair at the head of the table, which I presume is reserved for the High Lord, and load their plates, conversing quietly.

The human chatter dies down as everyone eats. After I have filled one of the flat breads, creating what can only be described as a fae equivalent to a stuffed pitta, I glance around at the others. They are all enjoying their food, especially after three days of travel rations. Although I liked them well enough.

To my left, Sascha and Mollie are whispering about something, I can't quite make out what, but it looks heated. I can't help but watch them, trying to decipher what is being said. It looks to me as if Sascha is trying to convince Mollie of something as they both cast glances up at the brothers. Eventually Sascha sighs, and Mollie faces the two high fae, expression determined.

"Which one of you was it?" She demands.

Silence falls over the table and all eyes dart between Mollie and the brothers. The air turns static with tension. Neither fae answers, but they glance quickly at one another. My gaze turns back to Mollie who is glaring down the table at them.

"The High Lord of Autumn told us one of the Lords

of Summer helped his brother open the portal that *dragged* us all here. Which one of you was it?"

The High Lords twin glowers at her, while the younger brother looks down at his plate, cheeks darkening in a flush.

"You then," Mollie accuses.

The smaller built brother looks up sheepishly, but is unable to meet her stare, his Adams apple bobs as he swallows. Eventually he nods, his brow creasing, before he looks back down at his plate.

"Why?" Mollie seethes, her voice pure venom.

"You do not have to answer her," the twin interjects.

"I think you'll find he *does!*"

"*No,* he does not."

"I was not allowed to speak to the Autumn Lord because he was imprisoned for what he did. Yet, here *you* are," she turns her attention back to the younger brother, "enjoying a feast with us, as if you have done *nothing* wrong. I deserve to know why you did it."

He looks up again then, eyes wide and watery. The tension in the room is as thick as honey.

"I… I'm sorry," he mumbles, standing and rushing from the room.

His brother stands, having watched the young Lord hasten from the room. He turns back to Mollie, his expression enraged.

"You would do well to remember that you are here as our guest."

"I am *here* against my will!" Mollie shrieks, also rising from her seat.

It is darkly fascinating to watch. Mollie is tiny; barely past five feet and petite. Yet she is standing up to the tall, muscular fae, like a mouse to a lion, as if they are equally matched. Charlotte, Edith, Sascha and I have stopped eating altogether to watch the spectacle.

"Then you should be grateful that the fae of this land

have taken you in, rather than leaving you to the wilderness, as I have no doubt *you* would not last an hour."

Mollie flushes scarlet before storming from the room. Sascha sighs and follows after her. "Mol, wait…"

"Excuse me," the Summer Lord speaks, his words clipped. "Enjoy the rest of your meal." He then turns on his heel and stomps away, heading down the same corridor as his brother.

"Well, that was awkward," Edith mutters sarcastically beside me, once the three of us are alone.

Charlotte and I snicker, and the humour cuts through the tension, which dissolves in an instant. We all giggle as I take another sip of sweet cherry juice. It's not funny really. Our being stuck here is quite serious, but the three of us seem to be on the same page: the fae have to send us back eventually, so we may as well enjoy ourselves while we are here. It's kind of like an extended holiday. An adventure.

"There was no need for Mollie to be that rude," Charlotte comments. "I get that she's angry but…"

"That doesn't excuse the way she spoke to the Summer Lords," Edith agrees, and I nod my head. "I know our being here is inconvenient, for them and us, but the fae have been nothing but pleasant… well Autumn Lady being the exception," another round of sniggers. "The High Lords twin is right; we should be grateful that they are treating us as guests."

"I'm actually really enjoying myself," I admit. "I was just beginning to feel the tug of wanderlust back home. I couldn't wait until my tenancy was up, so I can hit the road again."

"How often did you move?" Charlotte asks.

"It varies. Sometimes I'm quite content in one place for months, other times I'll feel the tug after a couple of weeks."

"Wow, up until we came here, I'd never even left the state!" Charlotte explains. "You?" She asks Edith.

"My parents used to take me to Austria every year, we would go skiing, and ice skating," she recalls with a fond smile.

Edith and I discuss our various snowy holidays, Charlotte listening eagerly with vicarious pleasure. For a brief moment I long to see the white snow-covered mountains, and feel the chilly breeze on my skin, but then I remember the view from my balcony. Something about being here feels right, like a homecoming.

I have the strangest sensation that, for now at least, this is where I am meant to be.

Chapter 9

High Lord

I wake with unusual vigour.

The High Lady of Autumn insisted on my company for much longer than I anticipated last night, and by the time I made my way to the banquet hall, the humans had already left.

Cursing, I had returned to my chambers, trying to expel my anxious energy. I had attempted to reply to correspondence and tried to read, but nothing could quell my racing thoughts. At one point I considered heading down to the guest wing, and seeking out my mate, but by the time it occurred to me I was sure she would be abed.

Instead, I tossed and turned all night. My thoughts wandering to the image of the blue haired female. She reminded me of my beloved Summer Court, her hair like the turquoise waves in the bay, her skin the same golden hue as the sands of the coast. I longed to know everything about her.

Eventually I fell into a restless sleep, dreaming of *her.* Her soft skin, warmed by the sun under my fingers, her lips against mine, the moans of pleasure she would make as I claim her…

Then I woke with the dawn, rising as the sun did,

eager to see her. I washed and dressed quickly, keen to make it down to the banquet hall, so that I might be there before the humans arrived. Perhaps I could even catch my mate alone.

When I reach for my chamber door and swing it open, a thrill of anticipation churning in my gut, I find my twin, hand raised as if just about to knock.

"Brother," he greets, his face indifferent as usual. "I need to speak with you."

"I am headed to breakfast," I tell him, in no mood for his complaints this morning.

"It's urgent."

With a groan I step aside and allow him to enter.

"I need to discuss the events of last night," he explains, standing uncomfortably rigid beside a chaise.

When I raise a brow at him, and the unwelcome irritation in his voice, he continues. "One of the humans was… vocal about her distaste for being here." My heart drops into my gut, is my mate unhappy? "The short one, with hair like a cloud."

I breathe a sigh of relief, and nod to my brother, perching on the end of my desk, indicating that he should continue.

"She questioned our brother and I, asking which of us was involved in the portal cleaving. While neither of us admitted to it, it was clear from our brothers face and body language that it was him. The human then proceeded to demand answers from him, having made no bargains, until he was so distressed, he ran from the hall. I… berated the human, then left them to comfort our brother."

"This report should have been brought to me last night," I scold.

"I know. But you were with the Autumn Lady, and by the time I had finished consoling our brother… it was late and I… I needed to clear my head." A strange expression washes over my brother's face, until he shakes his head and returns to his usual stoic self. "I walked along the beach to steady my thoughts, by the time I returned, I assumed you would have already gone to bed."

I consider how best to deal with this situation, rising and walking towards the balcony, my twin in tow.

"I will speak to the human… all of them. If it is answers they seek, perhaps offering them will assuage their hostility."

"It only seems to be the tiny one who is hostile," my brother explains.

"Either way, I'll speak to all of them." That way I have an excuse to speak to my mate alone. "I will check on our brother before I head down to breakfast."

"He already left."

I turn, my head tilted questioningly, as my brother crosses his muscular arms over his chest, his gaze not leaving the horizon.

"I passed him in the hall on my way here. He did not wish to dine with the humans this morning. Instead, he has ventured into the city. I sent a couple of palace guards to trail him—at a distance—to ensure he does not get into any trouble."

I nod my agreement. Although I dislike having my brother followed, he often thinks with his heart instead of his head and, evidently, makes poor choices. It is for the best that an eye be kept on him.

"Very well. I shall speak with him when he returns then." I turn away from the balcony, a view that never fails to steal my breath, and head back into my chamber. "For now, we should join the humans for breakfast."

"I will walk with you, but I shall not join you. I do not wish to… antagonize the angry little human again. I think it would be best if I kept my distance until you have spoken to them."

I bob my head. As much as the idea of being the only one to dine with the humans makes me uneasy, my brother is right. He is the less eloquent twin for sure and his grumpy presence alone may be enough to offend the human females.

"Very well," I concede, leading my brother from my rooms, and down the corridor towards the banquet hall.

We walk in silence, having never been ones to converse much—only when it is necessary. Even if my twin insisted upon conversation, I am not certain I would manage it this morning. My thoughts are far too occupied with my mate. I try to keep pace with my brother, but my feet seem as eager as the rest of me to be in her presence.

As we approach the banquet hall, my heart thumps relentlessly in my throat, my stomach churning with anticipation.

"I take my leave," my brother excuses himself, and before I can even reply he is already stomping away from the hall.

When I enter the room, the excitement that had been welling inside me disappears, like a wave receding from the shore. My mate is not here.

Only two females sit at the table; the short blonde my brother described, and the dark-haired female. Yesterday she was dressed all in black, and her clothing covered much of her body. Today she wears a Summer Court dress which reveals more of her skin, and I notice it is covered with strange colourful markings. As if someone has painted her.

"There should be five of you," I say once I am in earshot.

"Wow, someone aced math," the angry female snaps.

"*Mollie,*" her companion hisses.

"*What*?"

"The other three will be joining us shortly I assume,"

I add, ignoring the angry female's tone, and trying to keep the hope from mine.

"No," the painted woman informs me. When I raise a brow at her she continues. "Willow was up at the crack of dawn and took the others with her to explore the city."

Disappointment floods my body. I have missed her again. "I do not know which one Willow is," I remark, wondering why the humans are giving up their names so easily.

"Blue hair…jangles…stoner," the blonde—Mollie—grunts as she chews on her omelette.

Willow, that is the name of my mate. I do not know what a *stoner* is, but I remember her soft azure hair, and the gentle jangling sound she made as she moved curtesy of her many bracelets. I fight back a grin, and cling to this crumb of information.

I fill my glass with cherry juice, then select my breakfast: a slice of toasted bread with eggs and tomatoes, and a small bowl of fruit with yogurt and honey. All the while I recall the brief moment that I saw her; it fills my chest with longing and anticipation, but I must be patient.

I eat, letting the silence stretch out, as the two humans finish their meal, glancing at each other occasionally. When my plate is clear I rest my elbows on the table, interlocking my fingers and consider my next words carefully.

"I understand you have questions."

The two females meet my level gaze.

"Yes," Mollie tells me bluntly.

I nod. "Very well, I will speak with each of you—"

"And will you be as elusive as the High Lord of autumn?" She interrupts angrily.

"No," I answer, "You may ask your questions and I will do my best to answer them."

"No bargains?" The painted female asks.

"No bargains," I confirm.

"Thank you," Mollie grumbles reluctantly. Her companion thanks me as well, although she seems more sincere.

"I will leave you in peace," I inform them as I rise from my seat. "I shall be in my study until midday. You may come and ask your questions at your convenience, anytime throughout the morning. Any of the palace staff will be able to direct you."

I politely bob my head, then leave the banquet hall. The moment I cross the threshold I hear intense whispers, but I ignore their words. I have offered to answer their questions without a bargain. There is little else I can do to assuage their dissatisfaction.

Their frustration is understandable—their anger. Though I would prefer if it were not directed at my brother. As much as he had a part to play in their arrival here, he acted under the influence of another. It would never have been his intention to cause another distress; his heart is too kind, too gentle. I will not allow the humans to harass him for answers.

As I pace down the marble columned corridor, I let my mind wander back to my mate. I pulse with the desire to track her down, to see her again, to discover the sound of her voice. I consider heading into the city and doing just that, but I must be patient. It is unlikely that humans know fae customs…

When I enter my study, I push down the current of excitement rolling through me. *All in good time.* I have waited this long; I can wait a few hours more for her. For Willow.

Chapter 10

Willow

Summer Court is breath taking.

Too excited to sleep, I woke with the sunrise and eagerly sought out Edith and Charlotte, dragging them into the city with me. I say city, it feels more like a quaint Greek village, with whitewashed walls, aqua blue roofs, pale grey paved roads, and ornate fences attempting (and failing) to contain the most beautiful bougainvillea I have ever seen. It reminds me of when I spent a summer working in a vineyard just outside Mykonos.

"Oh look!" Charlotte gasps beside me, pointing to an iridescent hummingbird, flitting between magenta blossoms and I smile at her discovery.

Edith links her arm with mine and leads the three of us down another street, this one lined with small shops, each vying for our attention.

One vendor sells colourfully painted pottery, another sells jewellery made from shells. Edith points to a stall offering garments made of the most beautiful silks, all in colours of the ocean, everything from deep midnight blue to the palest pastel shade that reminds me of the foam that crests a breaking wave.

We pass artisans and craftsmen and women, overwhelmed by the colours, and sounds of the bustling city. I can't help but notice though, that each stall only holds a minimal amount of stock, and every so often we pass a shop that is empty or closed.

Eventually we find ourselves in an open square with an ornate marble fountain in the middle. The central column has been sculpted to look as if water is erupting from the center, and sparkling sprays splash down into a mosaic pool below.

Around the edge are smaller, temporary stalls with brightly coloured awnings, selling all manner of foods: bowls of olives, breads, cheeses, glass jars of honey and oils, cured meats and rows of succulent looking fruit. Chickens cluck around a pen in one corner and I can see a couple of goats tied to posts.

But again, although the variety is bountiful, the quantity of any given item seems low… as if it were the end of tourist season.

As we draw closer to a stall with lots of little baskets, all containing small mounds of herbs and spices, I spot a familiar figure bartering with the vendor for a raspberry pink powder. Without thinking I approach him.

"Last week you only charged me three," he insists.

"Yes, Lord, but I cannot get any more, what you see there is the last of it. Five."

"Please don't call me that," he beseeches gently. "I understand, I will pay four."

"I will accept," the vendor agrees, tipping the last of his pink powder into a pouch and handing it to the young male.

"Hello," I chime once coin has been exchanged.

The Lord turns to me, his youthfully handsome face paling when he sees me. "You're the High Lords younger brother."

"I am." His eyes dart nervously from me to Charlotte

and Edith, who I can hear behind me, trying to guess some of the less familiar fruit.

"Don't worry, Mollie isn't with us."

He frowns at me, and I can't help but chuckle.

"Mollie is the one who gave you a hard time at dinner yesterday."

"I know," he tells me in a small, uncertain voice. "I'm just confused why you are being friendly. I thought you all..."

"Thought we all hated you for bringing us here?"

He nods.

"Nope," I reassure him. "I'm actually having quite a bit of fun being here and Charlotte and Edith there are... well, they want to go home, but they aren't having a terrible time. They aren't mad at you."

Something in his expression shifts and he looks at me with a little sparkle of hope, then glances over my shoulder at the others.

"What's the pink powder?" I ask, pointing to the pouch in his hand.

"Oh, its beetroot powder. Mostly its used in food, but... I have been trying to make a dye out of it, specifically for... well for hair."

"Hair?"

"Yeah," he chuckles, rubbing the back of his neck awkwardly. Well, isn't he the cutest?

"Have you ever made blue hair dye?" I ask, seeing an opportunity.

"Uh, no."

"Perhaps that could be your next project?" I suggest, twirling one of my curls around my finger. "Mine is due a touch up soon, it would be awesome if I could keep it blue."

His warm brown eyes light up at the challenge, and he nods. "Sure."

I grin widely at him as Edith and Charlotte come up

either side of me. He watches them both carefully.

"I was just telling the High Lord's brother here that we don't hate him," I explain.

"Hate you?" Charlotte asks in disbelief.

When the Summer Lord nods, I'm glad that both women agree with me.

"Of course we don't!"

"We were told it was an accident, bringing us *all* through," Edith continues. "It's… inconvenient, sure, but all the fae have been perfectly accommodating. We aren't all as angry about it as Mollie is."

"I'm pleased," he smiles.

I like this fae, he seems sweet. An idea springs to mind.

"I don't suppose you would be willing to be our tour guide, would you?"

All eyes turn to me.

"We have been wandering around for a couple of hours now, and we are keen to see the beach. I could see it from my balcony, but this city is a maze."

"It would be my pleasure," the fae lord grins. "This way." He pockets the pouch of beetroot powder and leads us away from the market square.

We meander through the narrow streets, as our tour guide points out certain landmarks so we can find our way to and from the beach by ourselves next time. The sound of gulls, and the salty tang to the air increases as we draw closer to the coast, and finally we are led out onto a wide paved promenade.

I stop in my tracks. My breath caught in my lungs. Sapphire waters glitter all the way to the horizon, while the golden sand of the crescent shaped bay, stretches out in both directions, until it is intercepted by the high white cliffs that surround the city. Overhead, a cloudless sky creates a canopy of the most perfect blue. It's so beautiful my eyes prick, and my throat tightens. I can't put my finger on why but arriving here feels like a homecoming.

"Um, guys…" Charlotte pulls me from my thoughts, and I follow her gaze to the handful of fae enjoying the beach.

"Oh my god!" Edith gasps, her hand rising to her mouth, to stifle a giggle. "It's a *nudist* beach!"

"Uh, why is everyone naked?" I ask our tour guide.

"So, they do not get their clothes wet," he replies, as if the answer is obvious.

"Fae don't have swimsuits?" Edith asks, receiving a frown. "You know, clothing especially for bathing in the sea?"

The Summer Lord stays silent, his gaze flicking between the three of us, and the beach revellers.

"Yeah, I don't think the fae have swimsuits Edie…"

"Oh man, I was really looking forward to a swim," she complains.

Charlotte stands beside me, her expression mortified. I turn to watch the fae playing in the gentle midday waves, a banquet of body shapes and skin tones, all enjoying themselves, not one caring that they have *everything* on display.

"Well, I'm not opposed to a bit of nudity," I announce, "But maybe for today we could just go for a paddle?"

Edith gives an eager nod beside me, while Charlotte remains silent. I link my arm with hers and lead her towards the ocean. Once we cross the wide walkway, I reach down and remove my flip flops, practically jumping into the sand. The fine grains are warm against my bare feet, and I hum with enjoyment, wiggling my toes. I drop my flip flops and bag on the shore, grabbing the bottom of my skirt and tucking the hem up in the waist band, so that the longest tendril of fabric brushes my knee—luckily, we all wore Summer Court floaty dresses today—and I race down to the water.

We get a few odd looks from the fae already in the sea, who are clearly unaccustomed to seeing clothed bodies, let alone those that belong to humans, enter the water.

"Oh, it's so warm!" Edith exclaims as she steps in beside me, holding her skirt up.

The balmy water laps at our ankles and I grin from ear to ear. The sea is so clear, I can see tiny fish darting around us. I turn back to see that Charlotte hasn't joined us, she lingers on the beach, looking at Edith and I nervously.

When I wade back over to her, she is chewing on her lip, her eyes dewy.

"You ok?"

She nods but looks over at the fae frolicking in the waves just down from us. Then she glances down at herself, running hand over her tummy. *Ah.*

"Hey," I speak softly, squeezing her by the shoulders. "I'm not sure these fae are ready for the glory that is your thighs… maybe we should ease them in, and just give them a little calf for today huh?"

She giggles, blushing, then gives me a little nod.

"May I?" I ask reaching for her hem.

When she nods again, I pull one side of her skirt up. She is wearing the two-tone wrap around dress from yesterday, which doesn't have a waist band, so I knot one side of the skirt just above her knee, then the other side up by her hip, making sure the fabric still flows down the length of her thigh.

"There, perfect!" I announce, taking her by the hand and dragging her towards the water.

She lets out a little squeal when I don't stop and keep charging even when we reach the sea, tugging her with me until we are almost in up to our knees.

"Oh, it *is* warm! It's like a bath," she exclaims.

"This is peculiar," the Summer Lord declares as he comes to stand beside me. He has rolled his trousers up to his knees and looks down at the waves lapping gently at his toned calves.

I can't help myself. I reach down and splash water up at the fae male. He gasps and looks at me in shock even as I giggle.

"That's for bringing us to the *awful* place!" I laugh.

More water douses him, and I look over to see Edith bent at the waist, her hands in the sea ready to strike again.

"Yeah, this place is *horrid*, how could you?" She teases.

Realisation draws on the Summer Lords face, and he reaches down, swiping his hands through the crystalline water and flinging it up at me, then Edith. We both squeal and return fire.

"Help us Char!"

Charlotte wastes no time, reaching down into the water and dousing the male between us. He puts up a fight, the pleasant rumble of his laugh cut off when Charlotte splashes him in the face.

"I yield. I yield!" He cries, raising his arms, a beaming smile on his face.

"Ha! You humans are mad!" He bellows, enjoyment lacing his words.

I look around at our surroundings, once again taken back at the sheer beauty of it. Raising my hand to shield my eyes from the sun, I look up at the cliffs. The view from up there must be amazing and I make a note to venture up there at some point. Probably on my own, so I can write in my journal, with that incredible view.

"In all seriousness," I say quietly to the fae next to me, "its stunning here."

"I'm pleased you are enjoying it," he tells me, tone proud.

We wade around in the shallows a little longer before our toes start to wrinkle and we make our way back up the beach. Sitting in a row, we enjoy the view, although Charlotte still looks a little embarrassed at all the naked skin wandering around.

The Summer Lord, converses with us easily. It is much nicer to talk to him, than any of the other fae I have met. While he doesn't ask us direct questions, he carefully structures his sentences to probe us for more information. Each of us takes it in turns telling him a bit about ourselves, and in turn he is open to discussing himself and his brothers.

Hours must pass, as we sun ourselves in the bay. I feel a calming contentment fill me as I listen to my friends talk and watch the tide lightly lap at the pristine sand with the sounds of the distant tumbling waves echoing off the surrounding cliffs. A gentle, warm breeze picks up as the sun heads for the horizon, and my tummy starts to grumble.

"We should head back," the Summer Lord tells us. "It will take a little time to get back to the palace, and we need to freshen up before dinner."

We all stand and dust ourselves off. I feel almost loathe to leave. Today has been wonderful, and back at the palace there is still a lot of tension. But at least we have managed to convince the young lord that we don't *all* hate him.

"I think we should come back tomorrow," I voice. Even if no one joins me; I will come here alone. I may even wander up to the cliffs. The thought of that, sitting high above Summer Court, smoking some herb, scribbling away in my journal, enjoying the view, fills me with so much anticipation I grin from ear to ear.

"We will," the Summer Lord assures me, excitement plain on his face. "Tomorrow my brother hosts his weekly beach party."

Chapter 11

High Lord

Two days my mate has been in my court, and I have yet to even speak to her alone.

Yesterday morning I missed her; she had already left to explore the city and I didn't see her again until she returned for the evening meal. She'd had that sun kissed glow about her that told me she'd spent the day at the beach.

I later found out that she had been accompanied by my brother. He had told me about his day with the three humans; how he had bumped into them in the market, how they had been kind to him, and asked him to show them the bay. Being the fae he is, of course he agreed and had spent his day playing in the tide and conversing with them. With her. With my mate. I don't begrudge my brother a joyful day, but I am envious of the time he has spent with her. Especially when I have only had glimpses.

At the evening meal, she had sat amidst the others and spoken animatedly about their day. I had absorbed every word that fell from her lips. Letting the energetic timbre of her voice soak into me.

I had hoped to catch her after the meal, but once

again, the Lady of Autumn Court had demanded my attention. *When was she returning to her own court?* I longed to speak with my mate.

Then this morning, the blue haired female had not even attended breakfast. I had sat in the banquet hall from sunrise, until mid-morning, only to find she had already ventured into the city again. *Was she avoiding me?*

Duties that I couldn't shirk had kept me busy for the rest of the day, had kept me from wandering into the city myself to find her. Longing muddied my thoughts, and I'm certain I got nothing done efficiently. All I could think of was her.

Finally, my duties were done, and it was time to head to the beach for the weekly party. It seemed frivolous to still be holding them when my court was on the brink of ruin, but they kept the spirits if my people up. It gave them something to look forward too. For some it was even an opportunity; the bards and musicians that entertained, the vendors that provided refreshment, some merchants even tailored their wares specifically for the event. It did the economy good. I just wasn't sure how much longer they could continue.

My sandals clack against the paving as I make my way to the shore. I can already hear the pounding of the drums, and the energetic tempo matches that of my heart. It beats wildly in my chest as anticipation churns in my gut like a maelstrom.

The narrow path gives way to the promenade, and I am greeted by a party in full swing. Several bonfires have been lit along the shore, and everywhere I look, I see fae dancing and drinking, full of life and energy.

Overhead the sky is streaked with pink and orange as the sun starts to drop beyond the horizon, casting a golden glow over the waters of the bay.

Stretching my shoulders, to ensure my wings are

positioned proudly, I head towards the throng. Fae stop their revelry as I pass to wish me well and welcome me. I nod and respond politely but do not linger with anyone for long. I am keen to find my mate.

I find my twin quickly, in his usual perch by the fire. Tonight, he is bereft of attention, and is instead glowering at the short blonde, and painted human as they dance. I can't understand why he despises them so.

"High Lord!" Someone cries behind me, and I spin, hoping it is my mate.

It is not.

The Lady of Autumn Court comes staggering towards me, a slender red-haired female clinging to her hip. I stifle a groan. I have no intention of spending another evening at her disposal.

"I just wanted to say thank you," she slurs, the female beside her giggling. "It has been so long since I was able to enjoy myself." She wobbles, sipping from her glass before righting herself.

"Now if you will excuse me," she begins, pausing to snicker as the red head nuzzles at her neck, "I have some autumn summer relations to attend."

"Enjoy yourself, Lady." I bob my head.

With that the two females stumble away, chortling, and groping one another clumsily. I let out a grateful sigh. For this evening at least she will not require my company.

A young male approaches me after a few minutes of wandering through the crowd, a circular metal tray in his hand laden with small glasses filled with brightly coloured liquid.

He offers me the tray with a slight bow, and I oblige, taking a glass containing a bright green liquor. I tip the drink down my throat, enjoying the gentle burn, and the fresh minty flavour that settles on my tongue, then return the glass.

I continue my search, weaving through the mass of fae, convinced the entire city has gathered this evening. As I head towards the next bonfire, I spot my younger brother. His crown of springy coils bounces as he dances, his smile genuine and his eyes sparkling with excitement.

As I make my way toward him, I realise he is not dancing alone. He is with the other three humans. He is with my mate. I have found her. The joy of seeing her overwhelms me and halts my approach. I cannot simply stroll up to her. *Can I?* In the past it has always been the other way around. Fae have sought me for my attention, their intentions clear. But this is different. This is my *mate.*

I decide to wait a while. To gather my confidence. It does not usually leave me feeling so bereft, but in her presence, I feel like an inexperienced youth again. Perching on a rock, close to those who are dancing, I reach for another drink as a fae passes me with a tray. This one leaves a citrusy tang on my tongue; the gentle haze of the alcohol eases my anxiety a little.

But still, I do not venture closer. She has not seemed to notice me, so I admire her from the short distance between us.

Her gently tanned skin glistens in the firelight, and her eyes, like the bangles she wears, sparkle. As she spins and twirls her skirt whips around her legs, and I notice that she is bare foot. *How well she already fits in to my court.*

It takes two more songs before I can wait no longer and build up the confidence to approach her. I ease my way past those dancing between us, mindful of my wings and step up beside her. She is mid spin, and she barrels straight into me.

"Oh! Sorry," she giggles, still enjoying the music and dancing.

"No problem."

I can't stop looking at her, the shape of her face, the curve of her brows, the angle of her nose, the softness of her lips, the fine sheen of sweat shimmering along her collar bone.

"Dance with me?" The question tumbles from my lips before I can stop myself and I grimace. We have not bargained for questions—

"Sure!"

To my surprise she wraps her arms around my neck and starts swaying her hips, gyrating to the thump of the drums. Grinning up at me, she tilts her head back as I take hold of her waist, and her turquoise locks tickle the back of my hands. I hold her gently and attempt to match her movements, but they are jarring and unpredictable, as if she is completely lost in the music. Cautiously I pull her a little closer, my heart pounding, and move to one side, leading her steps, trying to encourage a more rhythmic pattern.

She leans further back, and I grip her hip to stop her falling. When she rights herself, her face is so close to mine, I can feel her breath on my skin. I can see her long pale lashes and the captivating silvery depths of her eyes, even if the silver is barely visible, as her pupils are so wide.

I can feel her breasts pushed up against my chest, and the rise and fall of her heavy breathing. I cannot move. I have my mate in my arms, and she is staring at me with such intensity that I am pinned in place.

My mate swallows, then, before I realise what is happening, she tiptoes and slams her lips into mine. My grip on her instantly tightens, as I press my mouth to hers, claiming her. She hums, and parts her lips, allowing my tongue to sweep in and caress hers. Her hands snake around my neck as she kisses me fiercely and passionately. It is as if I am the bonfire, utterly aflame, lost in the feel of my mate in my arms.

Her hands suddenly press against my chest, and she pushes, pulling out of my arms abruptly, spinning away from me. For a second my heart drops into my stomach. *What have I done?* But then she doubles over and vomits, splattering the sand.

I quickly reach for her, sweeping her hair back, holding it out of the way, and wrap my arm around her waist to stop her from toppling. She groans and sways, before leaning towards me. I help her straighten and lead her away from the drumming and dancing. She presses her hand to her head as I guide her down onto a rock.

"Sit for a moment," I encourage.

Her head rolls forward, her eyes drifting closed as she sucks in deep breaths. Crouching beside her, I rub her back. I cannot help myself; she is my mate, and she is unwell, it my duty to take care of her.

"Oh shit! Willow?"

One of the other human's dashes over. She is of a similar build to my mate, but her hair is a golden blonde instead of blue. And where my mate's eyes are silver, this females are dark brown, almost black.

"Willow, are you ok?" She asks, crouching.

"She is sick," I explain.

"Probably too much to drink, I'll go get her some water."

With that the other female rushes away. I return my attention to Willow, my heart giving a thump at the knowledge of her name. I continue to stroke her back, eager to comfort her.

After a few minutes, her friend returns with a water and kneels in front of her.

"Here, Will, drink this."

Willow raises her head a little and her friend tilts the glass to her lips. My mate sips from the glass before pulling away, rivulets of water trickling down her chin. I itch to wipe them away, but I restrain myself.

"I want to go home," she whines, and I don't know if she means home to the human realm, or home to the palace, to her bed…

"We can't go *home* home just yet, but I can take you back to the palace," her friend comforts.

"I just want my bed," Willow sniffs.

"I'll take her," I announce a little *too* quickly.

"I'll come with you."

"No" I say more forcefully than I intended. "You should stay and enjoy the party. I'll make sure she is safe."

The human chews her lip for a moment in consideration, watching me as I rise, clearly unsure if she can trust me to care for her friend.

"I will take good care of her, you have my word," I promise, though I don't know how much weight my word has with the humans. Among the fae it is unbreakable. Eventually she nods and stands as well.

I reach down, wrapping one arm around Willow's shoulders and the other under her knees. After tilting her back gently in an attempt to avoid making her feel nauseous, I haul her up against my chest. She makes a gentle groan at the movement, but as I settle her in my arms, she leans into me and relaxes.

The other human watches as I carry Willow away from the party, I feel her eyes on me, but she does not follow. Eventually I cross the promenade and turn a corner into the city. I am out of sight. With a sigh I retract my wings, trying not to grimace at the uncomfortable sensation of their absence.

Instead, I focus on Willow. She lays across my arms, her face relaxed, her breathing even. This close I can see her pale lashes fanning her cheeks, the softness of her lips as they part slightly. I glance lower, at her breasts, watching her chest rise and fall as she breathes deeply…

my cock twitches beneath my skirt and I look away.

As I make my way through the city, my mind wanders back to our kiss. The feel of my mate in my arms, of her body pressed against mine. The way her lips felt, the sensation of her tongue dancing with my own. My cock throbs again and I groan. *Fates.* Now is not the time for this. I take a deep breath and will my body to calm.

Finally, we reach the palace, and I make my way through the empty marble halls to the guest rooms. When I ease Willow's door open, I find that her bed is unmade, which I am grateful for as it will make putting her in it a lot easier. I ease her down onto the sheets gently and she whimpers a small protest at the movement, but then curls up and settles. I draw the light blanket up to her waist and crouch beside the bed.

"Sleep well, my pretty mate," I whisper.

I cannot help myself. I reach out a tuck a soft azure curl behind her short rounded human ear, a smile tugging at my lips. She is so beautiful; I wish I could stay here and watch her sleep all night, if only to stay in her presence longer. Of course, I decide against it. With a sigh, I stand, and am pleased to see that there is already a jug of water and glass on her bedside table.

There is nothing more I can do. I have upheld my promise, so even though I am loathe to leave her side, I know that I must. As I head for the door, I steal one last glance at her before I leave. *My mate.* A smile tugs my lips. I close my door softly and allow my mind to wander once more. I think of our future together and my thoughts swim with the possibilities. As I stride down the corridor to my own rooms, I plan for tomorrow. My duties can wait, I wish to spend the day with my mate instead.

Chapter 12

Willow

There are builders using jackhammers in my head I'm sure of it.

I don't open my eyes because I can feel the bright sunlight just beyond my lids and decided I don't want it. My mouth feels like it's full of sand and my body feels like I have been hit by a truck.

The need to pee presses on my bladder urgently, and I know I should drink something, if only to wash away the sand, but I can't quite bring myself to move.

Wait… how did I get back to the palace? The last thing I remember is—

Knock knock!

I groan as my head throbs painfully and manage to grip the corner of the blanket, pulling it over my head to block out some of the sunlight. *Ah, that's better.*

The knock sounds again.

"Go away," I grumble.

"Willow. It's me." A deep rumbling male voice tells me. I know that voice… The High Lord.

I pull the blanket back down, aware that my hair now resembles as birds' nest. *Why is the High Lord here?*

"I wish to check on you," he tells me through the

door.

Um, okay. "Sure… come in!"

The door opens, and the High Lord enters. Was I complaining that my mouth was dry? It's watering now. He's wearing a sand-coloured pleated skirt, and a sleeveless tunic, which fits his muscular body and compliments his dark skin perfectly. His locs have been pulled back and coiled at his crown, highlighting the structure of his face and… where did his wings go?

He grins as he crosses my room, then comes and sits on the bed beside me, his weight dipping the mattress. I groan at the movement. My words are lodged in my throat as I look at his brown eyes that shimmer gold in the sunlight.

"Good morning," he says quietly with a smile that sends my insides fluttering.

"Good morning," I reply, my voice hideous and raspy.

"You do not seem yourself," he observes.

"No shit."

I look down at myself, and notice I am fully clothed. I pinch my vest top, examining it for I'm not sure what and frown.

"How did I get back?"

"I carried you," the High Lord tells me. "After you were unwell."

"Unwell?" Then it all comes flooding back. "Oh God!"

The hangover haze clears just enough for me to be horrified. I had made the rookie error of smoking some herb *before* drinking, snogged the High Lord, then vomited on the beach. My hands snap up to cover my face before it turns crimson.

"I'm so embarrassed."

Gentle hands pull mine back to my lap, and when I look up, I am met with a soft gaze.

"You needn't be. Not for vomiting, and certainly not for kissing me." There is a warm expression on his face that eases some of my mortification.

"I hope you don't mind me checking on you, only the others have all been for breakfast, and you weren't there, so..."

"No, I don't mind."

It is only then that I realise he hasn't let go of my hands yet. In fact, it is at that very moment that he rubs his thumbs over the tops of my wrists, tiny little circles that make my skin tingle.

"I was hoping that if you are heading into the city again today, I could accompany you."

I swallow hard. Here I am, looking like I have spent a night in the wilderness with hair a tangled mess, and probably puke breath, while *he* is up in here looking all Greek-statue-esque, wanting to spend the day with me. How's a girl supposed to say no?

"Sure," I say, my voice more of a whisper than I intend. *What has gotten into me?* "Let me just freshen up."

I pull my hands away from his, feeling oddly bereft at their absence, then reach over to the bedside table and pour myself a glass of water. *Why is it so hot in here?* I down it, then turn away and clamber out of the other side of the bed. My head is *not* happy. It throbs irritably as I stand and stagger towards the little bathroom that adjoins my room. I haven't been this hungover since I spent New Year's Eve in Sydney a few years back.

Plumbing is a commodity I will always be grateful for. I turn the faucet and splash my face with cool water, drying it with a towel, then chew one of the little minty tabs kept in a small glass jar by the basin to clean my teeth and freshen my breath. I pee as quickly and quietly as I can, not wanting the High Lord to hear me, then tug off last night's clothes, replacing them with a pale coral dress that is made of the softest floaty fabric. A gift from the Summer Court.

Feeling a little more human, I emerge from the bathroom to find the High Lord looking quizzically at my phone which is sat atop the bedside table.

"I'm guessing you have never seen a phone before," I giggle.

He only shakes his head.

"It's a communication device primarily, but it also holds photos—images—and does all manner of things but… well it stopped working when we arrived here. I take it out to check occasionally, but it is always a blank screen."

"Ah," he acknowledges, but I get the distinct impression he doesn't know what I am talking about.

I reach for my bag and rummage around for some painkillers.

"Shit, I think I've run out," I huff, tossing my bag back on the bed. "I don't suppose fae have painkillers, do they?"

"I don't know what that is," the High Lord informs me, an apologetic look on his face.

"Little white tablets, pills that stop headaches, ease sickness, help with pain—"

"Ah! Yes! Here."

The High Lord reaches into a pocket and pulls out a small glass vial with a yellow liquid in that looks suspiciously like pee. He offers it to me excitedly.

I take it from his hand cautiously. "What's this?"

"A tonic, it will settle your stomach, and stop your head from aching."

"Really?"

He nods with a grin as I pull the cork stopper out and warily sniff the potion. It smells astringent and spicy. Throwing caution to the wind I tip the vial to my lips and pour it down my throat. It doesn't taste that bad, reminding me of strong ginger tea and turmeric. Instantly the haze in my mind begins to clear, and the gurgling in my tummy ceases. My muscles regain their composure and feel limber, then my headache disappears entirely.

"Wow, this stuff's amazing!"

The High Lord gives a proud smile, "I'm glad I was able to help."

"You could make a killing with this in the human realm!" I exclaim, but the High Lord looks distraught.

"I do not wish to kill anyone."

"Ha! No, silly. It is a human phrase; meaning to be successful."

"Oh," he frowns, clearly not understanding the idiom.

"Okay, shall we?" I ask, suddenly full of energy.

The High Lord nods, and gestures for me to lead the way, so I all but skip from the room and head down the hall. I have gone this way every morning thus far, so I know where I am going. I stroll confidently down the corridor, aware of the regal male behind me.

We cross the marble lobby and exit out onto a cobbled courtyard. At the far side is a high arch way with an open lattice gate. The sun warms my skin as we leave the palace grounds, making our way through the white-wash buildings, and the warm breeze feels wonderful, fluttering my dress around my body, and makes me feel all tingly. I can already hear the gentle roar of the waves and smell the faint fragrance of seaweed. Fae bustle about, focused on their daily business. Some push carts holding various supplies, some hurry past with their children in tow, whose tiny little pointed ears poke out from their unruly hair. I can't help but grin.

"You are enjoying yourself in Summer Court," the High Lord states.

When I turn to face him, he is smiling too, clearly

pleased to see me appreciating his court. "Yes, it's beautiful."

"I think so," he agrees. I watch him for a moment, as his brows furrow, and his lips twitch as if he is trying to work out how to say something but coming up short.

"You know you don't need to bargain for questions with humans, right? We ask and answer them freely."

His gaze shifts to me. "I did not know that."

My grin widens. "Yep. No need to trip over your words, if you wish to ask me something, just ask. I will answer."

He licks his lips and looks contemplative for a moment, before settling on his first question. "How does Ethea, Summer Court, compare to the human realm?"

"Well, um, the human realm is pretty big. The landscape is diverse, so I mean, yeah, there are places similar to this in certain parts of the world. There's, mountains, forests, deserts, huge cities, entire continents made of ice."

"And you… you have been to all these places?"

I chuckle. "I wish! It would take several lifetimes if not more to visit all the places in the world, but I have seen more than many. That's actually what I do… my job. I travel to places and leave reviews—stories about the places I have been, so others can decide if they wish to visit there too."

He nods his understanding as we step out onto the promenade. I sigh, looking out across the bay. It is breath-taking. The sky overhead is without clouds, a clear perfect blue, and the water sparkles like glitter under the midday sun.

Kicking off my flip flops and carrying them, I step onto the warm sands and start walking along the beach. The High Lord matches my pace, walking easily beside me quietly contemplating. After a moment I feel his fingers brush the back of my hand, then slide down my palm and interlace with my own. I should let go. I know I should, but his hand is warm and feels *right,* as if it is supposed to be there. My cheeks heat and I know I'm blushing, but I try to ignore it as we round a corner, past a small outcropping of rocks to a section of beach that is vacant.

Once we are out of sight of any onlookers, the High Lord stops, giving a gentle tug of my hand, pulling me to face him. My breath catches in my lungs as I stand in front of him. His golden-brown eyes are fixed on me, pinning me to the spot, and I am struck by how handsome he is. I admire him for a moment, his strong brow, his broad nose, and pillowy lips. I recall what it was like to kiss them and suddenly ache to do so again.

"I am happy to be here with you Willow," he tells me, his hand coming to my cheek, thumb caressing gently.

He leans towards me slowly, tilting his head, eyes fluttering closed at the last minute. Soft, full lips brush against mine and I shudder at the tenderness of it. I suddenly feel all hot and bothered, so I rest my hand on his chest—wow—and pull back before my knees buckle. He watches me carefully, concern flickering in his eyes.

"How about a swim?" I ask, eager to cool down.

When he quirks a brow at me, I take a step back and reach for the tie of my dress, fingers fumbling with the knot. Finally, I manage to loosen it, and shrug the garment off. It isn't until I am stood bare in front of him, that I realise what a bad idea that was. His eyes roam over me, and I feel exposed in the most titillating way. Shoving my trepidation aside, I turn and strut down to the water (swaying my butt as seductively as I can).

I turn back to the High Lord only to discover he has already stripped. Miles of gloriously dark skin and rippling muscles and—*fuck*—I can't help but look at his package. My mouth waters at the sight and I quickly turn away to launch myself into an incoming wave.

It breaks right over my head, pushing my unbound hair back. When I re-surface, I find the High Lord has swum out to me and is treading water at my side. With a grin that sends my tummy fluttering, he overtakes me and starts swimming out to deeper water. I follow, matching his strokes. The water is crystal clear, and I can see schools of fish twirling beneath me. Absently I wonder if Ethea has other aquatic life such as whales and sharks… I've always wanted to swim with sharks. I have always loved swimming in the sea and relish the feel of my muscles remembering the movements with ease.

"Where are we going?" I call out after a few moments.

"I want to show you something, just past Turtle Rock," the High Lord explains, pointing to what is indeed a large rock poking out of the waves in the shape of a turtle.

As promised, we swim just past it and back towards the cliffs. We approach land, and I notice a cave opening partially covered by a waterfall. The High Lord swims straight for it and pauses right in front of the cascade of water, turning to face me.

"Close your eyes," he commands.

I do as he says, treading water and letting my eyes drift closed. As soon as they are shut, I feel his hands take mine.

"Deep breath," he instructs, right before he pulls me forward, under the waterfall. The icy water splatters my skin and I grin, trusting the High Lord as I feel the air cool, and the sound of rushing water echoes around me. I follow him for a few more moments, until he stops me, and I feel him swim behind me, holding onto my waist.

"Open your eyes," he whispers in my ear, sending a shiver that has nothing to do with the cool air along my skin.

I obey, and a gasp escapes me. We are in a large cave. Along one side is a wide ledge of rock leading to the back where there is a crescent of sand, a hidden cove. Holes in the rock overhead allow beams of light to dapple the space, and where the mist from the waterfall permeates the air, the light refracts creating a canopy of rainbows.

"This is my favourite place in my whole court," the High Lord tells me. "I wanted to share it with you."

A strange feeling sweeps over me, honour at being shown something so special, but also something deeper, as if this means more than I can quite comprehend.

I turn to face him and am met with a molten gold gaze, and an expression of wonder. But he is not admiring the cave. He is looking at me. My insides flip under his observation, and my pulse quickens.

This time when he leans into me, I embrace my desire, drawn to him like a magnet. My arms wrap around his shoulders, dragging him closer until our bodies are flushed. Then our lips collide in a consuming kiss. Greedy desperate kisses that leave me panting. His grip on my waist tightens and a ragged sigh leaves me as his mouth claims mine. He tastes like honey, and I can't get enough.

I gasp when my back hits rock and I realise I am pressed between the High Lord and the rocky ledge. Without thinking I wrap my legs around his hips, all too aware of his erection pressing against my backside.

"Willow," he grits out, before devouring me again. "I need to taste you," he tells me, and I nod, right now I would agree to anything.

I release a squeal as he hauls me up onto the ledge, but I lean down so that I can continue to kiss him, tangling my fingers in his locs. He holds the back of my neck, as the other hand caresses my thigh, then pulls his mouth away from mine. I whine at the absence, but it is quickly replaced with a moan as his mouth captures my nipple, sucking firmly. My head rolls back as I hold his head to my chest, his tongue and teeth working the pert peak in a way that has me gasping for air.

His mouth leaves my breasts, instead trailing kisses down my stomach. With a gentle push he eases me back, so I am laying on the rocky ledge, it is smooth, cool, and flat under me as my knees hang over the edge, my feet still in the water. His lips brush along my inner thigh, feather light.

"Your hair is blonde here," he observes.

"Did you expect it to be blue?" I tease with a giggle, which is cut off and replaced with a gasp when he drags his tongue between my folds.

The High Lord groans as he sweeps his tongue over me again and I buck as it catches my clit. My thoughts short circuit and I can't think about anything but his mouth on me, completely unphased by the fact that he has me spread open on a rock as he devours me. I grip his shoulder, my other hand still curled into his hair, blissfully enjoying the way he lavishes me.

My moan echoes around the cave as his mouth wanders, his tongue circling my entrance. A small voice in the back of my head acknowledges that I don't even know this males name, but the thought is quickly forgotten when his tongue dips inside me.

"You taste incredible," he growls against my hot slick skin.

"Don't stop," I beg, lost in the carnal pleasure of having him between my thighs.

He redoubles his efforts, his tongue returning to my clit, circling it with a precision I didn't know males possessed. Then I feel his finger dragging along my center, coating his fingers before teasing my entrance. I let out a guttural cry as he slides his finger into me. He glides in and out, twisting slightly to create the most delicious friction, then adds another.

I'm spiralling, utterly lost in delirious pleasure as he coaxes me closer and closer to the edge. Panting, I rock my hips against him, chasing my release, I'm so close.

"Willow," he groans against me, the vibrations of his voice making me quiver. "My Willow… My mate."

Wait…What?

The cloud of euphoria stutters, like a vinyl record scratching. What did he just say? My climax dissolves into nothing as I sit up, pushing him away. He looks up at me, eyes glazed over.

"What did you just say?" I demand.

"I… I said *my Willow, my mate."*

"Mate?" I repeat.

Realisation sweeps over his expression as I push him back further, shuffling to the edge of the ledge and easing myself back into the water.

"Yes, mate."

"No, no, just because we've kissed, and you did… *things*… doesn't make me your mate," I explain, paddling a little to put some distance between us.

"Willow you… you *are* my mate."

"No, I'm not," I insist.

"Then how else do you explain the connection?" he asks, hurt lacing his words.

"What connection?"

He stares at me a moment, the pain in his eyes deepening. "You don't feel it? The tingling heat between us? A desire stronger than you have ever felt before, eluding rational thought? The magnetic pull towards one another?"

Shit, that's what that is?

"No…" I whisper, my words lacking conviction.

"Willow please…" he swims towards me, hands reaching, but I pull back.

"No, I… I can't be your mate."

"But—"

"No," I tell him firmly. "This was a mistake."

I turn to swim away, but his hand catches my arm, and he pulls me to him.

"Willow, wait," his voice is desperate.

Spinning to face him, I steel my resolve. "No. I'm not your mate, I don't *want* to be your mate."

I see my words hit their mark, slicing at him as he winces, his grip loosening. "Willow," he whispers.

"Let me go."

He hesitates for a moment, but I stare him down. His eyes search mine for something, but when he doesn't find it, his face contorts in anguish, even as his hand falls from my arm and he gives the slightest of nods.

Without another word, I swim towards the opening of the cave, the waterfall crashing over me as if pelting me with reality. I don't look back. Instead, I will my body to forget the throb still aching between my thighs, to ignore the tug in my chest to return to him, and swim as fast as I can back to shore.

Chapter 13

High Lord

My mate has… rejected me.

Water laps at my chest as I stand watching the waterfall she swam through, the shock of what has just happened immobilising me. My heart races, the thump of it deafening, but with each beat I feel it crack.

I look around, as if searching for hope. What was once a sacred place, a cave of beauty, now feels tainted. I cannot stay here, this place no longer holds any joy for me, it is the place where she told me she didn't *want* me. Recalling the words is like a knife to my heart and I grimace.

Finally, I will my body to swim, despite the pain in my chest. I emerge from the cave and head back to the beach. All the while my entire body aches, but not with exertion. As I round the rocky outcropping, the small cove comes into view, and I spot Willow walking through the shallows. She strides out of the shoal and scoops up her dress, tugging it around her body then storms away down the beach. She will be gone by the time I reach the shore and I long to call after her, to beg her to wait, but I doubt very much that she would heed my words.

Confusion gnaws at my thoughts. Why does she reject me? Is it me? Am I not good enough for her? Or does she simply not wish for a mate? No, that can't be it, who would not want a mate? They are the greatest blessing from the Fates.

My feet touch sand and I stomp back to my pile of clothes, my footsteps heavy. I dress then march back through the city. If anyone acknowledges or speaks to me, I do not notice. My mind is consumed by thoughts of Willow. How am I lacking? What is it she wishes for in a mate that she cannot find in me?

When I reach the palace and cross the cobblestone courtyard, I find my twin stood in the entranceway, waiting.

"A word, brother," he says as I approach.

"Not right now," I huff, in no mood for conversation.

I continue past him, earning a scowl, but he follows me down the hall.

"I know you do not wish to discuss Winter Court, but their actions cannot go unpunished. While their attacks do not reach us, Spring and Autumn need our support."

"You're right, I do not wish to discuss it."

He falls into step at my side, and I feel his gaze on me. I do my best to ignore him.

"Something has happened," he assesses. "You seem… troubled."

A grunt is all I manage as I barge into my study, pacing over to my desk and pouring a glass of wine. When I look up my brother has closed the door and stands rigidly waiting for me to speak. I know him, as well as I know myself, he will not leave until I offer him an explanation.

"She rejected me." The words fall from my lips and wound me all over again.

I watch my brother's brow furrow, a question lingering in the air between us.

"Willow," I elaborate, sitting at my desk. "The blue haired human, she is my mate. I took her to the cave beyond Turtle Rock and…"

"A mating bond has never been rejected—"

"I'm well aware," I snap, attempting to wash down my despair with a swig of wine.

Slowly, my twin crosses the room and sits in the chair opposite me, his posture softens, and I would find it comforting if it were not so unnerving to see.

"I know you will not want to hear my candour," he begins. "But I do not think a *human* is a fit mate for a fae."

"Explain."

"They are weak, they have no magic—"

"*We* barely have any magic, we are just as weak, if not more so than them."

My twin shakes his head, disagreeing.

"We know from our historical interactions with the humans, that they have short lifespans. No fae should want to bind themselves to a mate who will pass within a handful of decades, when we live for centuries."

"Yet we don't," I argue. "As the magic of Ethea dies, our existence shortens. Our father was barely one hundred and fifty when he returned to the fates. Besides, surely even a handful of years with a mate is preferable to a lifetime alone."

His expression flickers, as he readies to counter me, but a knock echoes through the room. We glare at each other a moment.

"Enter!" I bark.

Our brother pokes his head into the room. The innocent contentment on his face fades as he is exposed to the tension in the room.

"I am interrupting… I shall return later."

"No, you wished to see me, speak," I demand.

He glances between me and my twin, still hovering in

the doorway.

"Oh I… um… well… I just saw Willow return, she looked upset."

I try not scowl at his words; her unhappiness is my doing.

"I saw her leave with you… and then she returned without you and…"

My brother rubs the back of his neck, his gaze on the floor as he stumbles over his words.

"I have been toying with new dyes and paint. Willow expressed a need for blue—for her hair, and I think I have achieved it so… I um… I thought I could offer it to her, perhaps that would cheer her up. I could maybe even offer dye to the others… they have such fair hair, the dyes would work wonderfully, and I would like to win over Mollie, she is still angry—"

"Fine," I agree more abruptly than I intended. "I think Willow would appreciate your efforts. I cannot say for the others though."

My brother grins, the excitement plain in the glimmer of his eyes. Across the room my twin scoffs, and my gaze darts to him. Of course, he disapproves. I raise a brow at him, waiting for him to voice his discontent.

"You cater too much to the humans. They are ungrateful of our efforts."

"You have made no effort brother, you cannot possibly make that assumption," I argue.

With a grunt he stands, face twisted in anger. "You should send them back to Autumn Court and you know it. You would agree with me if not for one of them being your mate!"

He storms across the room, barges past our brother and stomps down the hall. My younger brother stares at me, face full of confusion. I sigh, taking another swig of wine before leaning my elbow on the desk and resting my head in my palm. I hear my brother's soft footsteps as he walks towards me, then he gently places his hand on my shoulder.

"I will listen brother, if you wish to talk," he tells me softly.

I peek up and meet the warm brown of his eyes. He is youthful my brother, perhaps a touch naive, but that does not mean he is foolish. He certainly has a far brighter outlook than my twin. Maybe he can offer some insight.

"Willow is my mate," I tell him, unable to hide the sting in my voice. "I took her to the cave beyond Turtle Rock, and when I told her… she rejected me."

He withdraws his hand and walks around my desk to sit where my twin had moments ago. When he looks at me, I can see the questions behind his eyes.

"Tell me what she said, exactly," he encourages.

I try to recall the precise words. "I called her my mate and she seemed… shocked. At first, she denied it, but when I explained, she said she could not be my mate, that she… she didn't *want* to be…"

"Perhaps the humans do not have mates," my brother muses. "Maybe they do not understand what a blessing the mating bond is. It does not sound as if she has rejected *you,* but that she is opposed to being mated at all. There has to be a reason for that. No one would turn down such a blessing from the fates." He speaks with the confidence of youth, then frowns, considering, before continuing.

"You could approach her differently. Get to know her, bargain with her for questions—though I doubt you would need to, the humans seem quite comfortable asking and answering questions. Find out more about her, then you may discover what she is looking for in a mate, or why she does not want one. It may not be anything to do with *you,* brother."

Perhaps my brother is right. Willow may not know how fae mates work, how much of a blessing they are.

"That is good advice," I admit. "I will approach her tomorrow, see if she will discuss the matter with me. I'm sure your gift will make her happy, and hopefully more inclined to talk with me."

My brother nods, rising from the seat. "I will do my best to put her in a good mood for you." His eyes twinkle with challenge and I cannot help but smile.

"Thank you," I say, my voice dripping with gratitude.

"I wish to see you happy," he grins. "Both of you."

With that he leaves, closing the door gently behind him. The silence of my office feels thick and heavy, yet I have not entirely abandoned hope. My brother's words have swelled my determination. In the morning I will seek Willow out again, and I will explain to her about fae mates. Once she understands what a blessing they are, surely, she will not reject the notion?

Unless it *is* me?

No, I cannot think like that, or I will be consumed by despair. That cannot be the reason. The fates would not send me my perfect mate, only to have her reject me. I have tasted her lips, and I have tasted between her legs, but it is not enough. I wish to claim her, to be with her always. We would not have crossed paths if that was not our destiny.

Surely the fates would not be so cruel.

Chapter 14

Willow

"What do you mean, *mate*?" Edith asks, her nose scrunching up in confusion.

"I don't even know," I reply. "But it sounded like… some sort of claim, like *ownership* or something."

Charlotte sits on the end of my bed, fiddling with the hem of her teal skirt. While Edith sits next to me on the chaise.

"It doesn't matter I guess, I told him he was mistaken. Just because he went down on me, doesn't make me *his*. I'm such an idiot, I shouldn't have gone to that cave with him."

"You didn't know he was going to go all possessive on you though," Char chimes in. "It sounded quite… romantic up until then. Skinny dipping and kissing and… other things."

I can't help but giggle. She's adorable.

"But was he right? Is there a bond? A connection between you?" Edith asks.

"I don't know. I mean, I guess, yeah. At first, I thought it was just the weather, you know. It's super-hot here, but remember when we arrived, and I thought the throne room was hot, but Char, you thought it was cool in there."

Charlotte nods.

"And then last night when I was drunk, I was all tingly when we kissed, and then I felt it again this morning when he was being sweet and checking on me, I honestly thought it was just because I had drunk and smoked too much." I sigh, frustrated with myself that I didn't notice before.

"And then, yeah, in the cave it was romantic, it was beautiful and felt like he had taken me somewhere special. Not to mention he's an amazing kisser… and *really* good with his tongue but…"

I shake my head, unable to explain myself properly. How do I tell them that now I have noticed the bond I can't ignore it? That I can't stop thinking about him? Or that for those few moments when things were magical, before they got weird, the connection between us felt stronger than anything I had ever felt in my life? That seeing my words hurt him, felt like a blade to my own skin…

My thoughts are interrupted by a knock at the door. Edith and I gaze at each other quickly, both worried it might be the High Lord.

"Who is it?" I ask the door.

"It's… me."

I giggle, recognising the voice of the younger Summer Lord. "Come in."

He pokes his head around the door, his face haloed with tight coils, a broad smile on his face. He is without a doubt the happiest fae I have met so far.

"I have made your dye Willow," he announces stepping gingerly into the room.

"You have?" I squeal excitedly.

His vigorous nod makes me smile. "I can bring it to you whenever pleases you."

"Is now too soon?" I ask eagerly, welcoming a

distraction.

The Summer Lord nods his head with a grin. "Now suits me."

"Oh, fun! I've always wanted to dye my hair, but never had the guts to do it," Char admits.

"I have other colours," the Summer Lord tells us. "Perhaps I could bring all of them. I would be happy to dye everyone's hair," he beams.

"I don't want mine dyed," Edith explains. "But Char, you definitely should!"

"Very well, I'll gather my supplies and be back in a moment."

With that the summer lord hastens away.

He returns a short time later with a reed basket practically overflowing with jars, bottles, boxes, and little paper sachets. Tucked under his arm are an array of towels and blankets and draped over one shoulder is a satchel.

I take the basket from him, noticing for the first time a band of scarring around each of his wrists and follow him into the middle of the room where we both sit crossed legged on a cushion. He hands me a bottle, the contents inside swirling in the exact same hue as my hair, then starts rummaging through the basket.

"There are many options for you Charlotte," he says without looking up. "Green, orange, purple, pink—"

"Oh, Char you would suit pink!" Edith squeals.

"I don't know, that's a bit… dramatic."

"Not all pink," the Summer Lord muses, now searching his satchel. "Perhaps streaks of a paler shade..."

Charlotte chews her lip as he pulls a bottle of pale bubble-gum pink dye from the depths of his bag and holds it up for her inspection. Her mouth curls into a smile and she nods her agreement.

"Excellent! Let me just get set up, I shall do yours

first, then Willow's."

Char grins excitedly and shuffles over to the Summer Lord, sitting cross legged in front of him. He digs in his basket again, pulling out an empty bowl and a wide bristled brush.

I take the opportunity to head out onto my balcony, grabbing my bag on the way. Taking up my usual perch with my back against the wall, and after stuffing the end of my pipe with herbs, I burrow around in my bag to find my lighter. I'm going to have to find an alternative as the fuel is running low.

I light the dried herbs, then suck in a lungful of the fragrant smoke. After a moment I release it with a sigh, enjoying the way my muscles relax, and my head starts to tingle. Closing my eyes, I listen to the sound of the waves in the bay, and the gulls overhead. The sun is already dipping, it must be mid-afternoon, and I feel the golden rays warm my skin. A gentle breeze caresses me and brings the scent of brine, salt, and something floral.

When I open my eyes, I glance out over Summer Court. I can see the ocean from here, the sun making the waves glitter and just before the horizon I make out the curved shape of Turtle Rock. With a huff I take another drag, remembering the events of this morning.

My mind replays them over and over; the swim, the kiss, his hands on me, his tongue… they race around like a whirlpool, and I can't seem to wrangle them into any sort of order. It's hard to regret any of it, though. I wanted to spend time with the High Lord, I wanted to kiss him, to do more. But… I don't want to be his mate. I mean—I don't really know what that means, but I'm sure I don't. It sounds… final. Like getting married, being tied to someone forever. Trapped. That's not me. I love my freedom, my adventures. I wouldn't give that up for anyone.

Time slips away from me and I'm not sure how long

I'm sat out on the balcony smoking, but the door slamming jolts me from my swirling thoughts.

"I've got snacks!" Edith calls, and I head back into my room, stumbling a little, my tummy grumbling.

I hadn't even heard her leave, but she is striding across the room with a tray in one hand laden with food, four glasses clutched in her fingers and a carafe under her arm. I reach for the glasses and help her lay out her provisions on the table. Just as I pop a dried apricot in my mouth, the Summer Lord comes to stand beside me.

"Your turn," he informs me with a warm smile.

Before I know it, I'm sat with a towel around my shoulders while the Summer Lord is applying an aqua dye to my hair that is the consistency of mayonnaise. He carefully rubs it into my hair, especially the roots, where he massages it into my scalp. I close my eyes and can't help the hums that vibrate across my lips at the pleasant sensation. It's easy to lose track of time when you're being pampered.

"We really need a name for you Mr-Summer-Lord," Charlotte declares, already a little tipsy.

She's sat on the rug opposite me, her hair streaked with dye, munching on a fruit skewer.

'Mr-Summer-Lord's' movements on my scalp slow before he answers her. "Only family and mates may know a fae's name."

"It doesn't have to be your *name*," she insists. "It could be a nickname or something."

"What about just your initial?" Edith suggests from the chaise. "Surely just the first letter isn't breaking any rules?"

"I suppose not," the Summer Lord agrees, rubbing the back of his neck. "My initial is 'K'."

"K!" Charlotte squeals. "That's so much better than 'Summer Lord'!"

We all laugh loudly at her overly enthusiastic

assessment until another knock at the door interrupts our merriment.

"Come in!" I yell.

The door bursts open revealing Sascha and Mollie. Sascha looks pleased to see us as she eyes the room eagerly, while Mollie looks pissed. Does she ever not?

I glance back at K. His excited expression falters as his gaze falls to the floor. I feel a stab of anger towards the arrivals when his brows furrow and he rubs the back of his neck nervously.

"What is going *on* in here? I could hear you down the hall."

"We're having a makeover party!" Charlotte squeals, causing Edith and I to giggle. Even K cracks a smile.

Mollie eyes the basket on the rug, then Char and I, before an opportunistic expression crosses her face.

"You have hair dye?"

"Yes," K answers, his voice uneasy. "Please, join us. If there is something—"

"Do you have bleach?" she interrupts.

K glances down at his basket. The air in the room thickens with tension. "I… I don't know what that is."

"Something that strips the natural colour out and makes it look like this." She points at her own hair, a chagrined look on her face.

"I… um…" K rummages awkwardly in his basket. "I might have something… or I could colour it… being that light, it would take dye well… I have blue, pink, green—"

"I don't *want* colour, I like my hair white-blonde, can you bleach it or not?" Mollie asks impatiently.

"I do not have *bleach*, but… I can make your hair stay whatever colour you want, for as long as you wish it. Here," he pulls a tiny glass bottle of shimmering powder out of the basket which reminds me of the inside of a shell and hands it to her. She takes it silently, frowning at him.

"What is this?"

"I conjured it a while back, it will make your hair appear as you wish to others and yourself."

Mollie raises an eyebrow suspiciously. "For how long?"

"As long as you like. The powder is enchanted, it will obey your desire. If one morning you wake and wish for hair like a cloud," he gestures to her head and she frowns again, "you shall have it, if you wish for blue like Willow's, it will be yours."

"Even if I wash my hair?"

The Summer Lord nods vigorously, a hopeful smile on his face as if he seeks Mollie's approval.

"It's the only bottle I have," he explains. "You will be the only one with the ability to change your hair at will."

Mollie looks down at the bottle, then back up at K, her expression softening. Eventually she cracks a smile, and I think it is the first time I have seen one on her face. "Thank you," she whispers, as if the words pain her.

K grins. "Please, join us," he encourages. "Edith brought wine and food."

"We should stay for a bit," Sascha adds.

Mollie glances around at each of us, looking reproachful. She mumbles something to Sascha, who sighs and grabs her by the elbow before dragging her towards the mound of cushions.

"Fine," Mollie agrees, dropping to the floor, and reaching for the crudites and hummus.

K spends some time with her explaining how to use the powder, and how to activate the enchantment—turns out it is all about *intention.* She doesn't press him for answers like she did at dinner a few nights back and I even catch her smiling again. Meanwhile, Sascha sits at the base of the chaise and chats to Edith and Char. I haven't really been paying attention to what they are discussing, but they are grinning and giggling.

It warms my heart to see them all getting along, especially K and Mollie, as I have seen how upset K was, thinking everyone hated him. I much prefer to see everyone happy.

It is at that precise moment that I realise I have never truly been happy. I thought I was, but it is a shallow sort of contentment that has never permeated me fully, only lingered at surface level. I am suddenly left with a strange, uncomfortable sense of unfulfillment.

I wonder what it would take to make me truly happy?

Chapter 15

High Lord

I watch as the sun rises over the chalk white cliffs from my balcony. I haven't slept. How could I? Yesterday my mate rejected me. The thought feels like water in my lungs, threatening to drown me on land.

Last night, at dinner, the humans were drunk on wine, they laughed and joked—even Mollie. Willow, with her freshly dyed, vibrant blue hair had seemed so happy with her friends that, despite my desperation to talk to her, I decided to leave her be. Instead, I watched her smile, listened to her laughter, and attempted to memorise every inch of her face, every curve of her body, every sound that passed her lips. All the while, the hollow feeling in my chest grew.

I managed to avoid spending the remainder of the evening with the Autumn Lady and snuck off to my room. I was keen to be alone, but once I achieved it, it only exacerbated my loneliness. All I could do was sit on my balcony and watch the sunset; the colours somehow muted. I'd watched the moon rise in the sun's place, and the birds swoop across the deep blue sky, envious. At some point I must have drifted off to sleep, because I woke, still sat on the chaise that adorned my balcony. I hadn't bothered getting up, or going to bed, I simply stayed there, until the sun began to rise.

Now it has fully risen, I need to decide what I'm going to do. I cling to my brother's words. Perhaps if I simply speak to Willow, and explain the bond, she will have a change of heart?

But if she rejects me again… I'm not sure my heart could take it, and part of me wants to distance myself from her, protect myself somehow. Avoid any further torment.

There is only one way to find out.

The pristine white hallways are cool as I trudge towards the guest rooms. My feet are made of stone, and my heart thumps in anticipation as my sandals clack against the marble, echoing off the walls. When I reach Willow's room I hesitate, hand raised ready to knock on her door. I take a deep breath and force myself to rap my knuckles on the wood.

"Come in."

I ease the door open and enter cautiously. I do not know if I will be welcome. Scanning the room, Willow is nowhere to be seen. Her bed is made, but the room is empty.

"Out here," she calls from the balcony, as if sensing my thoughts.

I cross the room and pause in the archway. Willow is sat to the left, her back against the wall as she looks out over the court. In her lap is a book, in which she is etching the view before her.

"I hope I'm not interrupting."

Silvery grey eyes dart up to meet mine, widening in surprise. She says nothing, just stares up at me, her pen paused on the page. My heart sinks to my stomach.

"I shouldn't have come," I admit. "I'll leave—"

"No." She sets down her pen, closing the book around it, her gaze cautious. "You're not interrupting."

She pats the tiles beside her, so I step over her feet and slide down the wall sitting next to her. We're not quite touching, but the sliver of space between us vibrates.

"What is this?" I ask, the question uncomfortable on my tongue, as I gesture to her book.

"My journal."

"May I see?"

"Sure." She passes me the book and I open it where her pen marks the page. I look at a sketch of Turtle Rock but decide perhaps I shouldn't read the words. *What if they are about me?* Instead, I flip back through the pages. There are leaves nestled between the ones where she has documented her stay in Autumn court. Further back are more notes in her scrawling handwriting and drawings of things I have never seen; unusually shaped buildings, vast landscapes, and fauna that we do not have in Ethea.

"These are all places you have been?"

Azure waves bob beside me as she watches me leaf through her journal. Some of the pages have things stuck to them; smaller pieces of paper with images on them, pressed flowers, coins. I pause when I come to a drawing of a ruin atop a mountain amid a valley.

"This… cannot be real," I mutter in awe.

"It is," Willow insists. "That's Machu Pichu, I hiked the Inca trail from Cusco to get there, it was breath taking."

My finger traces the shape of the valley, wondering what it must have been like to visit such a place.

"You have had many adventures."

"I have," her voice is soft, hesitant. "I hope to have many more."

I dare to glance at her, my brows furrowing. Her gaze lifts to mine, a determined sort of sadness in her silvery eyes.

"That is why you do not want a mate," I guess.

She sighs before nodding. "That's one reason."

I wait for her to explain as she pulls her legs up towards her chest and wraps her arms around them, resting her chin on her bent knees.

"I have always travelled. My parents were wanderers, always moving about. My birth certificate says San Diego, California, but I have no memories of growing up there. I remember learning to ski on the White Mountains and building snow men with my dad in Alaska. I remember learning to surf in the waves of Bondi Beach with my mom. I know how to navigate the London Underground better than most of the city's residents, and I can speak five languages—not fluently, but enough to order from a menu, or ask directions… What I'm trying to say is; travelling is in my blood. It's part of who I am… I … I'm not the sort of person to settle down. I'm never in one place long enough to have a serious relationship—let alone be someone's *mate*. Whatever that is."

Willow huffs out a long breath, as if exhausted, and looks out over the bay, not meeting my gaze. I understand now. She thinks I seek to take away her freedom. Even if she does not know what a mate is.

"You could have many adventures here," I tell her, my voice more of a whisper than I intend. She looks at me then. "There are four courts to explore, though I would advise against Winter, as they are not particularly hospitable. Ethea boasts beaches, deserts, meadows, and mountains. There are vast forests and… I do not seek to imprison you, Willow."

"You said I was *yours*, like I was a possession."

I shake my head, wishing I had not spoken when we were in the cave. My mouth was busy enough, I needn't have said a word.

"I do not consider you a possession," I insist. "I am

as much yours as you are mine, through the bond created by the fates. I would make you my High Lady, confidant, advisor, friend, and lover. My everything. As I hope to be the same to you."

"That still sounds like a cage to me," she sighs regretfully.

The gnawing ache in my chest sharpens and it is as if I have been speared with a trident. My lungs struggle to draw in breath. Truly she does not wish for a mate. I…I have met my mate and she does not want me.

The air between us grows thick and awkward as silence stretches out. I glance at the woman beside me who continues to look out over my court. Words lodge in my throat as I wrestle to come to the terms with the fact that I have lost her; I have lost my mate before I had the chance to claim her. Barely two days we shared; a handful of moments, but it is not enough, eternity with her would not have been enough.

What could have been lies in ruin around me. I should have kept quiet, I should have courted her, encouraged her to open her heart to me. I could have been patient, waited for her to feel at home here. Instead, I have scared her away. Fates, I thought the bond was enough, that *I* was enough.

"I do not seek to cage you, Willow, but give you the world," I murmur as I hand her back the journal.

She takes it and looks at me, her silvery grey eyes swirling with remorse. I cannot bear it. The way the sun illuminates her skin, the wave like quality of her hair, she steals away my breath and yet… I need to leave, to put an end to this torment. If I cannot be with her, then I need to distance myself.

"I take my leave," I tell her as I rise from the floor. After stepping past her I reach the threshold and pause. "I will leave you in peace. I hope you enjoy the rest of your stay in Summer Court."

Chapter 16

Willow

The High Lord leaves me sat on my balcony; his sudden absence makes my stomach knot. My chest feels tight, and a lump forms in my throat as I realise I'm… *sad* that he has gone.

I know I'm not cut out to be anyone's mate. I'm not that person. Despite the obvious bond between us, I could never commit to staying in one place. I have always valued my freedom and adventuring over anything else.

And yet… his words echo in my thoughts; *I do not seek to cage you, Willow, but give you the world.* What does that even mean? What does he really expect from me? A docile stay at home wife? No chance. I could never be happy tethered to one location. Travel is in my blood, without it I would be miserable, I know I would.

You could have many adventures here. He'd told me, listing all the things I have yet to see in Ethea. I find myself considering if this land could be enough to satisfy my wanderlust. His world seems so much smaller than mine. What if it's not enough? What if I stay and within a few months, a year, I have seen all Ethea has to offer, and nothing satisfies my need to adventure anymore? I'd be stuck here.

And then there's him. Sure, he's handsome, all dark skin and delicious muscles, as if he's been carved from onyx. But its more than that, there's a stillness to him, like the calm waters of a deep lake. I wonder what it would be like to get lost in his depths. Would they drown me? Douse my fire? Or would I float, weightless and free?

Opening my journal, I look down at my doodle of the cave the High Lord took me to and Turtle Rock, remembering how magical it felt. I had gotten so lost in him, in his kisses, his touches… I almost missed it. There was a part of me that longed for that again, for him. But that was just the bond, right? Some strange fae magic causing the constant ache that only lessens in his company?

I'm attracted to him sure (I mean who wouldn't be?) But the whole 'mates' thing really freaks me out. It seems so *final.*

With a huff I reach over and grab my bag, digging inside until I find my herbs. After stuffing the end of my pipe with the fragrant dry green leaves, I rummage around for my lighter. When I find it, I flick button and it gives a feeble spark.

"No, come on," I plead, working my thumb over the wheel. Nothing.

Frustrated, I stuff everything back into my bag and rise from the floor, slinging it over one shoulder. Maybe I can find a replacement in the market? Fae probably don't have proper lighters, but surely they have matches. I can work with matches.

I slip my feet into my flip flops and march out of my room, heading down the stairs to the large open foyer. As I stomp across the marble with determination I cringe at the slap of my shoes, and the way it echoes. I hope the High Lord isn't nearby, I can't think straight when he's around.

Outside the sun is high and the day is wonderfully bright. My skin warms, growing balmy in the delicious heat. Gulls squawk overhead and I can hear the faint roar of the ocean. It's oddly comforting to my raging thoughts.

I make my way through the city, easily finding the market. As I start to wander the stalls, anxiety crawls along my skin. What if I can't find any matches? I need the herbs to relax, and with all the thoughts swirling in my head, my need is greater than ever. What if I can't barter one of my belongings for them even if I find them? I have no fae coin, but I have a few things in my bag I could maybe trade?

"Willow!"

I turn to see K jogging towards me a beaming smile on his face which I can't help but return.

"Hi," I greet when he reaches me.

"Good day, I hope you are well."

"I will be once I find what I'm looking for," I reply. K raises his eyebrows questioningly. "I need a lighter… or matches."

The young Summer Lord frowns at me.

"Portable fire… for my pipe."

"Ah, for those strange herbs you smoke?"

"Yep," I agree with a giggle.

"Hmm," K contemplates. "I'm not sure about portable fire, but what effect do the herbs have? Perhaps I can offer an alternative."

"I smoke herbs to relax, especially when I am stressed."

"Ah… because of my brother."

"He told you?" I ask, suddenly embarrassed.

"He did."

"What did he say?"

K ponders for a moment, his lips twisting as he

considers his words. "Only that you rejected him."

His words feel sharp, even though his tone is gentle. I don't know how to reply. I did reject the High Lord didn't I. A strange wave of guilt washes over me and I remember the look of hurt in his eyes, the desperation in his voice…

"Come, Willow, I think I know of something that will help."

Without mentioning his brother again K leads me through the market to a stall selling vegetables and it is my turn to frown. While the produce looks familiar, none of it resembles anything I have eaten in all my travels.

After rummaging in his pocket, K produces a small bronze coin and hands it to the vendor. "Dried golden top please."

The vendor merely nods and reaches for a wicker basket containing weird grey shavings. They tip some onto the scale, then slide them into a small paper bag and hand them to K.

"Here," he grins at me, offering me the bag.

"What are these?"

"A type of mushroom."

Oh. Well, I have taken mushrooms before. I open the bag and pluck a slice out, holding it up to examine. When the light catches the crinkly slither of grey, I notice the curved edge is tipped in a shimmering gold. Makes sense, given the name. I worry my lip when I realise, I don't have any coin to pay K back. "What do I owe you? I don't—"

"It's on me," he smiles. "You're my friend Willow, I don't like to see you upset."

I return his smile. "Thank you." I pop a 'golden top' in my mouth. It's chewy and has an earthy flavour mixed with something else, a hint of sweetness, like powdered sugar.

"May I walk with you back to the palace?" K asks me. I'm oddly proud at how easily he now asks questions.

"Oh, I uh… I don't want to go back just yet."

I need to clear my head first. Get my thoughts in order. Besides, I don't want to run into the High Lord again, being around him only gets me more confused.

"I have been meaning to explore the cliffs," I explain. "I think I'll go for a walk up there, clear my head."

"Would you like company?"

"Thank you, but no… I want to be alone for a bit."

He gives me a kind nod, then reaches out and rests his hand on my shoulder, giving it a quick, comforting rub.

"All will be well," he reassures me, before turning and heading back up towards the palace.

I can't help but smile, he really is the sweetest.

With a sigh I turn, making my way out of the market and heading down to the beach. As I break free of the bright white buildings and step onto the promenade, a surge of joy washes over me like a wave breaking on the shore. I can't help but smile as I take in the wide stretch of soft golden sand, the shimmer of blue waters, the fishing boats with their colourful sails and the high chalk-white cliffs.

But like a wave, the feeling recedes. I have always loved the beach, the ocean, but the happiness I feel here… I don't trust it. I find myself wondering if it is heightened because of my bond to the High Lord. Would I feel such a powerful sense of… belonging without it?

I pop another couple of mushrooms in my mouth and chew on them thoughtfully. *How long do these take to kick in?*

With a nod of determination, I turn and follow the promenade along the bay. The light grey stones are sandy and make a gentle scuffing sound under my flip flops. At the end of the stone walkway, the path narrows to a gravelly trail that meanders out of sight.

I follow it, the small pebbles crunching underfoot, as it winds through tall cypress trees and course grass that scratches at the outer edges of my feet.

My steps carry me along as my thoughts churn. One step and I decide I don't believe in fate, and that I will leave when the time comes, and carry on living as I always have. Another step and I find myself considering staying, exploring Ethea instead, the handsome Summer Lord at my side. But then no, I'm not cut out to be someone's mate; he offers freedom now, but what happens when he is required to stay at court? Surely, he can't simply abandon his duties and wander the fae realm with me.

I chew on another mushroom as I reach the top of the costal path. A salty sea breeze rushes past me, whipping at my hair. It must have taken me longer than I thought to get this high because the sun has already begun to lower, it must be mid-afternoon already.

Even so, I keep going, my mind nowhere near clear enough yet. The path twists and I pace past fragrant gorse bushes. I watch them, as their bright yellow flower unfurl before my eyes, their pollen glittering the air. *Hmm, pretty.*

Looking out over the cliffs I can see Turtle Rock, the bright blue waters of the bay shimmer and make it look as if the turtle is swimming. I smile, starting to feel more at ease and reach for another mushroom. They must have started working because I'm beginning to relax.

A rustle from behind startles me and I whip my head around, but there's nothing there. It must have been the wind. I turn back the way I was going and frown as the sun is almost at the horizon. As I stare out across the bay wondering how *hours* have passed, something claws at my foot, and I yelp. But when I look down, there is only grass.

Another rustle, but this time when I look back down the path, I'm sure I see a shadow pass between the cypress trees.

"Hello?" I call into the dusk.

A loud screech sounds overhead, and when I look up, the clouds are churning furiously, dark and menacing. *I should go back*, I decide, but when I glance once again down the gravel path that leads back to the beach, I see more shadows, a dozen of them creeping between the trees. Squinting, I try to work out what they are, my eyes struggling in the fading light.

A terrifying roar rips through the air and I scream, searching for the source of the sound, but find nothing. Then I notice the shadows are drawing closer, and my skin prickles. My veins ice over as fear takes hold and I can't help the whimper that rises in my throat.

I can't go back the way I came, but I'm not safe, I know that with absolute certainty. When another roar pierces the air, eliciting another scream, I do the only thing I can think of. I run.

Chapter 17

High Lord

Willow isn't at dinner.

She must be avoiding me.

My twin sits to my left, stoic as always, barely concealing the glare he is directing at the humans. To my right, my younger brother sits with Charlotte, the fuller figured female who now has soft pink streaks in her hair. They converse easily, and I feel a spark of jealousy. I wish to speak with my mate in such a way.

At the far end of the table, the small female, Mollie, stares at her plate as she angrily stabs at her food ignoring everyone. Beside her the raven-haired Sascha is whispering fiercely with Edith. I know I shouldn't, but I try to listen in—perhaps they are discussing Willow.

"Ask him," Sascha hisses.

"Why do I have to be the one to ask, why can't you?" Edith replies.

I frown. What do they wish to ask? And of whom? Sascha glances at me, but quickly looks away, turning her attention to her friend, then quietly suggests something called 'rock, paper, scissors.' Edith groans but holds her hands out, her closed fist resting on top of her upturned palm. The two of the count to three, slapping their fists into their hands then both make a gesture. Edith holds her hand out flat, while Sascha holds out two spread fingers, a triumphant grin on her face. Edith huffs, then turns to face me.

"Um… High Lord, uh, may I ask a question?"

"You may," I nod, curiosity swirling below the surface.

"Um, well… we were wondering if you have seen Willow?" At my frown she continues. "Only, we haven't seen her since last night, no one can seem to find her, and we thought that since you were… well… you know…" She trails off awkwardly.

I briefly acknowledge that Willow has told the other females that we are mates, and feel a small pang of hope, but then what Edith has said sinks in. They can't find Willow. My mate is missing.

"I saw her this morning. She was… we spoke." I say cautiously. Not wishing to admit that our conversation hadn't exactly gone well.

"Then you were the last one to see her," Sascha informs me, as if I hadn't already worked that out. My pulse quickens, fear and anger colliding. My mate has been missing all day, and yet this is the first I have heard of it. I try to stamp down the panic, there must be an explanation. Willow is a free spirit perhaps—

"That's not… entirely true."

All eyes at the table turn to my younger brother, who looks down at his plate, his face solemn. When his gaze rises and meets mine, his expression turns sheepish. I quirk my brow at him, and he releases a shuddered breath.

"I saw her around midday," he admits, voice barely more than a whisper. His gaze darts around the room, guilt plain on his face. There's something he isn't telling me.

"Brother…" I snarl.

His gaze snaps back to me. "I… I gave her golden cap," he confesses.

"Please tell me you are lying," I grit, fury bubbling in my veins.

He shakes his head, his eyes watering.

"You will answer three questions," I growl at him. I will not bargain; he owes me answers for endangering my mate.

"I will," he nods, voice quivering.

"How much did you give her?"

"A handful."

"When?"

"Midday."

"And did you give her any instruction on how to take the mushrooms safely?"

"No…" My brother looks panicked as he tries to explain. "It was in the market; I gave her the golden caps and then she said she was going for a walk to clear her head. She didn't ask, she just headed towards the…" His throat bobs with a nervous swallow.

"Towards *what?"* I grit out another question, unable to control myself.

"The cliffs," he answers, hanging his head.

I clench my jaw so tight I fear my teeth may crack and rise abruptly from my seat. Without a word I leave the dining hall and pace back to my room. Ripping open drawers, I quickly find what I'm looking for; a small glass vial filled with a shimmering yellow elixir—the same elixir I had given Willow the day after the beach party. I storm to the balcony, my heart pounding like a drum on bonfire night.

Without thinking my wings erupt in a flurry of sparkling white feathers and I surge into the sky. I have to find my mate.

My wings carry me high above my court, the beat of them matching the pounding of my heart. I dart across the bay to the cliffs, scanning the rocky pathway that winds along their edge.

Overhead the stars are twinkling, the moon a glorious glowing crescent and there is a soft, warm breeze. I would enjoy them all, flying for the first time in years, if it weren't for the panic flooding my veins.

It's only a matter of time before my magic runs out, and my wings fail me, I must find Willow before then. I must ensure she's safe. Desperation tightens my throat as I glide as quickly as my wings will allow along the cliffs, frantically seeking any sign of her. What if I don't find her in time? What if my magic withers and I fall to my death before I have found my mate?

There.

A shock of blue hair, illuminated by the moonlight, catches my eye and I swoop down towards her. I land with a thud, my sandals skidding along the compact chalky ground, and I rush to close the distance between us, dropping to my knees at Willow's side.

She sits huddled against a rock, hugging her knees, weeping. When I reach for her, resting my hand on her shoulder she shrieks and cowers away from me.

"Willow," I say gently.

Her gaze whips to me, her eyes wide with terror. A ragged breath leaves her just before she flings herself at me, clinging to me as if her life depends on it.

"They're everywhere!" She sobs. "I tried to run, but my stupid shoes, I couldn't get away!"

Shifting my weight, so that I sit with my back pressed against the rock, I pull Willow into my lap. She curls against me, gripping my tunic and crying against my chest, trembling. My heart seizes at her fear, and I wrap my arms—and wings—around her protectively.

"I've got you," I whisper. "You're safe."

When she continues to shake, I reach into my pocket, withdraw the vial, and rip the stopper out with my teeth.

"Here, Willow, drink this, it will make them go away," I encourage, handing her the elixir.

She takes it with trembling fingers before tilting her head back and swallowing the yellow liquid with one desperate gulp. The vial falls to the floor, and she clings to me once more. I hold her tightly against my chest, relief surging through me. *I found her.*

As I stroke her hair, I whisper words of comfort. "I've got you." Until her sobs die down, replaced by whimpers, then eventually silence. Her breathing evens out, and her grip on my tunic loosens. With a loud sniff she pulls away, wiping her damp eyes with the back of her hand.

"What happened?"

"My idiot brother gave you golden cap mushrooms." I can't keep the growl from my voice. "One or two has a calming effect, but any more than that can cause severe hallucinations."

"Oh," she sighs, then leans against me once more as if exhausted. Unable to resist, I tuck turquoise locks behind her delicate rounded ear and continue to stroke her hair gently. "How did you find me?"

"I flew."

She pulls away again and gazes at my wings, her hand resting against my chest. I wonder if she feels the thump of my heart against her palm.

"Can I touch them?" she asks, her voice full of wonder. A smile curves my lips and I nod. "Sure."

I stretch them out behind me, opening them wide and await her touch. She reaches for them, then pauses.

"Are they sensitive?"

"No more so than my arms, or legs," I tell her.

Delicate fingers brush along the fine feathers closest to my shoulder and I stifle a shudder. Did I say they were not sensitive? Perhaps it is because Willow is my mate that her touch feels like nothing I have ever experienced, intimate and wonderful. I'm almost afraid to breathe, not wanting this moment between us to end.

"They're beautiful," Willow sighs, as her hands explore my wing, stroking each feather. "So soft."

I watch her, my mate. The moon illuminates her light golden skin, and the stars above reflect the silvery grey of her eyes. Her expression is one of awe, and my heart clenches at the sight. She is perfect.

The bond throbs in my chest, I feel it vibrate through my body. A near painful sense of longing fills me. What I wouldn't give to keep her in my arms. The thought of a life without her churns my gut and tightens around my throat. I keep the torment from my expression, watching my mate with a gentle smile as she continues to stroke my wings, oblivious to my internal struggle.

Willow leans across me to stroke the other wing and in doing so presses herself against me. My gaze lowers to the gentle curve of her nose, her dainty chin. Then to the sweep of azure curls along the delicate curve of her neck, down to the swell of her breasts which press against the confines of her dress. I swallow the lump in my throat, my lust and cock stirring.

"We should head back," I explain, shifting, hoping she does not feel me stiffening.

Willow recoils her hand, her glance sliding to me with a hint of apology, and I regret speaking. "Of course," she nods, holding onto my shoulders and rising gracefully.

I stand too, hoping the pleats of my skirt hide the partial swell of my cock. My legs feel weak, and I stagger. With a deep breath I steady myself, then notice Willow's hand is on my arm. When I turn to look at her, her expression is concerned.

"I have used too much magic," I explain. "We may have to walk back."

Before she can answer I flex my shoulders and draw

in my wings. The ache of their absence is more painful than usual.

"We can't fly back?" she asks me hopefully.

"I'm afraid not. I don't think I have enough magic to make the journey back." I hate that I have disappointed her.

"Hmmm, I didn't realise your magic was finite."

I want to apologise, but then I would be in her debt… although I wonder if she knows that about fae? Not that I would even mind being indebted to her, but I've been avoiding apologies for so long, the words for one lodge in my throat.

We walk quietly for a while, side by side. A few times I feel Willow's fingers brush mine. It is because the path is narrow, not because she is reaching for me. The evening is mild and despite being late autumn, there is a gentle warm breeze drifting up from the sea rustling the gorse. The pleasant roar of the waves joins the chirping crickets and the soft crunch of pebbles underfoot as we meander along the coast path.

Willow looks straight ahead, her gaze is clouded, her brows subtly drawn as if she is deep in thought. Her fingers clutch at the bag that crosses her body and rests on her hip. Every so often I hear her bangles jangling. I find the sound oddly comforting. It means my mate is nearby.

"What would happen if you used up all your magic? Would you stop being the High Lord?" She asks me after a while.

"In a way. High Fae are such because their magic is concentrated. It manifests when the fae comes of age and is… focused. My ability to fly for example. That magic is then used to help power our court. Once the High Fae of Ethea were powerful enough that each court had enough magic to power the entire realm, but now we barely have enough for our own courts.

"Magic for a High Fae is… their life force, so when they use the last drop of it, they cease."

Willow gasps. "They die?"

"Yes."

"Is it only flying that drains your magic?"

"No," I reply. "Even simply summoning my wings takes its toll, but far less than flying, that's why I haven't done it in so long."

"That's why you don't always have your wings out?" She asks, glancing in my direction.

I nod.

"How did you know you had enough magic to fly up here and find me?"

"I didn't," I tell her honestly.

"You… didn't? You mean you could have died?" Willow stops walking and turns to me, her lovely face contorted with concern.

"I couldn't have lived with myself if something had happened to you."

"But you could have *died!*"

"I know." The words leave me a soft whisper.

Willow stares at me, her gaze searching my face for something, and I can't tell if she is angry or upset. I don't want her to be either. I want her to curl up against my chest like she did earlier or kiss me passionately as she did when we went to the sea cave. But it seems the fates have other plans.

Willow's mouth opens, as if to speak, but then she closes it. She huffs out a breath then turns from me and continues down the path.

The rest of the walk is made in silence. My mate wraps her arms around herself as if she is cold, even though the air is still temperate and doesn't speak a word to me.

Finally, we make our way through the city, our footsteps echoing off the white walls of the long-deserted streets. Guards greet us at the palace gates, and we pass into the enormous marble structure.

The halls are empty as it is well past midnight and I assume everyone else is abed. Still not wishing to leave Willow's side just yet, I escort her to her room. She pauses at her door and turns to me.

"I don't like that you risked your life to save me," she complains, crossing her arms over her chest and *glaring* up at me. I press my lips together to stop a grin forming at her concern.

I'm not the only one who risked my life today. Willow was so intoxicated by golden cap that she was hallucinating creatures chasing her. She told me she had tried to run from them, and my mind still balks at the thought of her toppling from the cliffs in an attempt to flee. Of course, she isn't entirely to blame, my brother had a hand in it, but I will deal with him tomorrow.

Naturally, I say none of this to my mate.

"Your safety is important to me, as it should be to you. I do not regret my actions."

She looks down at her feet before responding.

"I don't usually endanger myself. I hate being a damsel in distress…" She fiddles with the strap of her bag then continues. "I'm grateful that you saved me, but I feel awful that you *had* to."

"I didn't *have* to, I chose to," I insist.

She scoffs, shaking her head, eyes still focused firmly on the floor.

"First, I get so wasted I puke all over you and you have to bring me a hangover remedy, then I get so high on mushrooms that I nearly charge off the side of the cliffs trying to outrun imaginary shadow monsters! You must be sick of me."

I can't help myself. I tuck my pointer finger under her chin and tilt her head up, so she is looking at me. The enchanting swirling silver of her eyes renders me silent for a moment until I compose myself.

"Never," I tell her honestly.

She stares up at me for a few moments, her gaze gradually softening. The tension leaves her brow, and the tightness in her jaw disappears. I'm so busy watching her expression that I don't notice her hands leave her bag strap and rest gently on my chest until I feel her warmth bleed through the fabric. She grips my tunic and leans up.

I suck in a breath and close my eyes just as her lips press against mine. I caress the soft curve of her jaw with my thumb and go to reach for her waist when her lips leave mine. *No.*

"Thank you," she whispers, her breath hot against my skin.

I dare not move, dare not breathe. The air around me feels fragile. I swallow, the sound loud in my ears, but keep my eyes closed. Willows lips no longer touch mine, but I can *feel* her closeness.

And then it's gone. My eyes snap open as Willow takes a step back, her expression unreadable. Her hands are back on her bag, and my chest feels cold in their absence, while my lips still tingle from her brief kiss.

"Goodnight," she says, her voice soft and ethereal.

My throat is tight, words eluding me. My mate turns, and hastens through her door, closing it swiftly behind her.

I don't know how long I stand there, seconds? Minutes? Her scent, earthy and warm, still lingers in the hallway and I breathe it deep, trying to assuage the ache in my chest. When the air clears, and the tingling fades from my lips, I finally find my tongue.

"Goodnight, Willow."

Chapter 18

Willow

Gulls squawking on my balcony drag me from my already fitful sleep. I roll onto my back with a grumble and look up at the carved marble as the terror of shadows, claws and teeth starts to ebb.

My thoughts instead conjure feathers, muscles, and kisses and I sigh at the pang of longing I feel. It isn't real though, it's just the bond making me think that it is. Tricking me. I don't really want to stay here, I don't want to kiss the High Lord again, and I certainly haven't thought about what it would be like to have sex with him. Nope.

Damn, my brain's a mess.

I get up and dress, then hunt down my bag and rummage in it for my pipe, then remember I didn't solve my lighter problem yesterday. *Shit.* I have some mushrooms left… no, that's not a good idea. Stuffing the pouch and my smoking gear back in my bag I pace the room trying to decide what to do. I could venture into town again, try and find some matches? But the thought of exploring today makes me feel weird, I think today I should stay in the palace. I have to do *something* though, or I'm going to go crazy.

Then I remember the pool room I passed a couple of days ago and decide that I will go for a swim and relax in there for a bit.

I sneak down the hallway, conscious of every turn. The last thing I want is to bump into the High Lord. I know it's childish hiding from him, but I'm not ready to face him again, especially after yesterday.

"Hey, wait up!" Someone calls when I am about halfway to the pool. I turn with a smile—recognising the voice—to see Charlotte speed walking to catch up. She links my arm immediately and we continue on our way.

"Ugh, this heat is killing me," she complains. "You're so lucky you don't get chub-rub, I swear it feels like I have sandpaper between my thighs."

"Oh sweetie, why don't you join me for a dip in the pool, that might help?"

She stares at me with disbelief. "Well for starters I don't have a swimsuit."

"So? Wear that, or get in naked, the fae aren't bothered by nudity, and you know what they say, when in Rome and all that."

"Yeah sure," she scoffs sarcastically. "It's alright for you—miss skinny dipping with the High Lord—you're built like a gazelle or something, all lean limbs and toned skin."

I give her arm a squeeze. "You only live once Char, so do what makes you happy. Don't let the narrow-minded opinions of others steal away your joy."

She frowns, but doesn't answer, as if contemplating her options. I continue towards the pool, content in the silence. As we round the last corner, I chance a peek back at Char and try not to smirk when I see a glint of determination in her eyes.

We pass under a marble archway into the pool room. The pool itself is larger than my entire apartment back home and lined with shimmering mosaic tiles in blue, white and gold. At the shallow end, two sets of steps lead into the enticing looking water. At the deep end is an ornate marble waterfall, which fills the room with a gentle trickling sound.

Around the edge of the pool there's seating, and tables, loungers and raised plant beds boasting small olive and palm trees. It's an idyllic room that has me smiling and prompts the strange feeling of 'belonging' again.

I grab two towels and walk alongside the pool. Edith is already in it, swimming leisurely towards the waterfall. She turns as she hears us approach.

"Hi!" She greets. "You have to come in, its divine!"

With a grin I kick off my flipflops, dump my bag beside the towels and tug my dress off over my head. Then I jump into the pool with an excited squeal. The water is cool, but not uncomfortable, just refreshing.

When I surface, I take a few long breast strokes towards the waterfall then lean back into the cascade of water scraping my hair back away from my face. I'm suddenly reminded of my time in the cave with the High Lord. The way the water spray glistened with rainbows, and the way *his* mouth felt against mine, against my breasts, between my legs… the way my moans echoed—

"Char are you coming in?" Edith shouts, pulling me from my thoughts.

I swim back over to where I left my things and find Charlotte hoisting up her skirt and placing herself on the pool's edge, her legs in the water.

"I'm working my way up to it," she admits.

When I reach her, I prop my elbows up on the side of the pool and rest my cheek on my forearm, so I'm facing her.

"So, what happened yesterday?" She asks.

"Wow, cut straight to the point why don't you," I reply with a playful grimace.

"We were all worried about you," Edith adds as she joins us, taking up the same position as me, but the other side of Char.

"Well, I was still freaking out about the whole mates thing, especially after the High Lord came and spoke to me yesterday morning, so I went to have a smoke, but my lighter has run out. I wandered into town to try and find a lighter or matches or something, and I bumped into K. He said he didn't know where to get them, but that he had an alternative. So, he gave me these weird mushrooms, which had a gold edge to them. I've done mushrooms before, so I thought nothing of it. Anyway, I went for a walk up to the cliff to clear my head, accidentally took too many of the mushrooms and ended up hallucinating being chased by shadow monsters."

"Oh my gosh!" Edith exclaims.

"Yeah, it was pretty scary." I pause while I remember the awful hunted feeling, and the imagined sensation of claws tearing at me. "Anyway, the High Lord swooped down and saved the day. He gave me the same tonic he used to clear my hangover the other day and held me… comforted me until it passed. Then we walked back."

"Why didn't you just fly back?" Char asks.

"Because he doesn't have much magic, he… he risked his life flying up to try and find me. He could have used the last of it and it would have killed him."

"Killed him?"

"Yeah, apparently when a High Fae's magic runs out they die."

Both women stare at me for a moment. I'm still angry at the thought of it. Angry that he risked his life to save me. I couldn't have forgiven myself if he had died.

But then I remember how frightened I had been and how relieved I was when he showed up. I felt so safe when he pulled me into his lap, wrapping his arms and wings around me. I remember how he whispered words of comfort to me while we waited for the tonic to take effect and the hallucinations to stop. How he had let me touch his wings and how soft they had been. How warm and strong his body had been enveloping mine. How his skirt had been tented when we stood to walk back to the palace. Our goodnight kiss.

"Wow, he must really like you, to risk so much to ensure your safety," Charlotte says quietly.

"I'm sure he would have done it for anyone," I argue, but I see Char and Edith glance at each other sceptically.

"What are you going to do?" Edith asks.

I don't answer her right away. If she had asked me a couple of days ago, I would have been adamant in my response. Nothing, I'm going home—not that I have ever felt at *home* anywhere…except here. *Ugh!* But now I'm not so sure. I can't seem to keep away from him, and part of me doesn't want to. It's true that there is a bond between us, a magnetism. But it scares the shit out of me. He doesn't want a quick fling; this isn't like a holiday romance. This is *mates,* he doesn't want to be with me for a few months. He wants forever. Yet, the more I think about leaving, the more uncomfortable I feel, and I still can't shake the feeling of belonging here.

"I don't know," I answer eventually. "Can we talk about something else?"

"Sure," Edith agrees. "How about the weather? I for one can't cool down! I have spent every day either in this pool or in the sea and I am still melting. I am much more suited to a colder climate!"

Char and I both giggle at her dramatics. It feels good to laugh.

For the rest of the afternoon we swim, and snack on figs and olives. Eventually Char gathers enough courage to join us in the pool, whipping off her dress and slipping into the water even as her cheeks take on a cute rosy blush.

Once the three of us start turning into prunes, we wrap ourselves in towels and head back our rooms to get ready for dinner.

It was a pleasant afternoon, full of fun and distractions. But when I close my door, finally alone, I realise I'm no closer to figuring out what I'm going to do about the bond, and my ridiculous idea to stay here in the Summer Court, with the High Lord.

Chapter 19

High Lord

As I wait patiently for the palace guard to leave my study, I examine the letter on my desk. I recognise the seal before I peel it from the parchment; red wax embossed with two oak leaves. The sigil of the Autumn Court.

My heart sinks into my stomach. Have they found a way to send the humans back already? They can't have—it's too soon. I had hoped… I don't know. After saving Willow, things changed between us again. When I held her in my arms and comforted her, I was overcome with the rightness of her against me. She had even kissed me when we returned to the palace.

Yet since then, she has not sought me out. Perhaps she expects me to seek her instead, but I promised to give her space and I do not want to go back on my word. Despite the longing I feel simply to be in her presence again.

Ignoring the maelstrom in my gut I break the wax seal and unfold the letter.

High Lord of Summer Court,

I hope this letter finds you well. It is my greatest joy to inform you that by the fates design, one of the females pulled through the portal is my mate. She has accepted the bond and will be staying in Ethea as my High Lady.

In an attempt to assist her human friends feel more comfortable here, we are travelling to Spring Court with two of her companions, as we seek the assistance of the Spring Lords.

My mate also wishes to visit her friends currently staying at your court and as such we will be passing through on our way to Spring. We hope that you will welcome us when we arrive in three days' time.

If any of the humans currently residing in your court wish to venture to Spring, we are sure they will be welcome to join us.

Regards,

High Lord of Autumn Court

I should be happy for the High Lord of Autumn Court; I know I should. But I can't help the churning jealousy in my stomach. He has found his mate and she has accepted him. She is staying with him. The very same outcome I had hoped for when I met Willow.

Selfishly I wonder if I might glean some advice from him. Some way to convince my mate to stay. And yet even as I think it, I recoil from my own thought. Remaining in Ethea *has* to be Willow's choice. I promised I would not cage her or make her feel trapped.

In order to make good on my word I must give her the freedom to make that choice, even if it kills me. Her happiness means more to me than even my own. If she truly wishes to leave, I will not stop her.

I re-read the letter and a new question forms in my mind. Will Willow leave and go to Spring Court? If she seeks adventure as she says, perhaps she will wish to see more of Ethea before she returns to the human realm. The thought fills me with dread, and I wish there were some way I could prevent it. If the humans are to return to their own realm, I wish for Willow to remain here until then, until she takes my heart with her.

Swallowing my turmoil I stand from my chair, refolding the letter and head for the dining hall. My feet are heavy as I traverse the marble halls, my chest tight. The once comforting sea breeze that finds its way through the gossamer hanging in the windows now feels a threat, a zephyr intended to carry away my mate. Once I had hoped for forever with her, but when she rejected me, I resigned myself to weeks, maybe months… now it seems I will have only days left with her before she leaves. The thought is a gaping wound in my chest.

Laughter drifts out of the dining hall as I approach, and I slow my steps. I know that laugh. It is Willow's and already committed to my memory. Lingering in the hall for a moment longer, I listen to the sound, enjoying the ethereal timbre.

With a sigh I straighten, grateful that I am not required to present my wings at dinner as my magic still feels faint. I brace myself and stride into the hall with a confidence I do not feel and take my place at the head of the table. As has become common place, the Autumn Lady is absent, I imagine she is in the city with the fae I saw her with on bonfire night.

My brothers sit either side of my chair. My twin to the left, silently eating his meal, and my younger brother to the right, speaking rigidly to Mollie. I should listen in to see what they are discussing, to assess if I should intervene, but I find that I do not care. My mate is leaving.

Further down the table, Willow is speaking animatedly to the other three, who all listen to her intently.

"...She'd hidden it in the tequila bottle!" My mate exclaims, before all four women burst into laughter.

I pour myself a glass of wine and sip from it. When I consider the food before me, I find my appetite has deserted me. So, I wait for the laughter to die down, then clear my throat loudly, resting my elbow on the table and holding the letter up between my fingers.

"I have received a letter from Autumn Court," I announce, and the room falls silent.

"Are they sending us home?" Mollie asks without missing a beat, hope in her voice.

I shake my head, "No. Not yet at least."

Taking a deep breath, I unfold the letter and read it out. When I am finished, I can't bring myself to look up from the words, too afraid of what I might see in Willow's expression. Relief? Excitement?

"Our court cannot accommodate—"

"It can, and it *will,*" I interrupt my twin.

He scowls at me, slams his cutlery down on the table, then storms from the room. I turn to my younger brother first, who is glancing at the humans with innocent excitement. It is clear he enjoys their company. Beside him Mollie is frowning, but she does not look angry, more... concerned. Her gaze follows my twin as he leaves the room, her frown deepening once he is gone.

At the bottom of the table Sascha, Charlotte and Edith are discussing whether to go to Spring Court. Each list what they like and dislike about my court and speculate what it would be like in Spring.

Finally, my gaze falls on Willow. She isn't joining in the conversation with the others. Instead, she's poking at an olive on her plate, her expression pensive. I'm surprised. I thought the news would bring her joy, that she would leap at the chance to leave.

She turns towards me, her silver-grey eyes meeting mine and once again I am struck by how beautiful she is. I try to school my expression into neutrality as I take in her high cheek bones, the pout of her lips, the way her wave-like hair frames her face and the golden hue of her skin. Her delicate pale brows furrow and her lips part slightly, as if to speak but she remains silent. I watch her mouth, remembering the feel of it pressed against mine, how soft, warm, and inviting it was.

I will never kiss her again.

It is too much to bear. I rise more abruptly from my seat than I intend, bowing my head politely and make my excuse to leave, the reason tasting like ash in my mouth. My sandals smack loudly on the floor as I stride down the hallway eager to seek out solitude. I may as well get used to it now, for a lonesome future with no mate looms just beyond the horizon. My sorrow at the thought threatens to swallow me whole.

Chapter 20

Willow

The sun is high in the sky as I make my way through Summer Court. I pass the bright white homes with their turquoise tiled roofs and the colourful marketplace with determination. A warm breeze floats up from the bay, bringing with it the familiar scent of salt and seaweed, rustling the bougainvillea, and adding a heady floral note to the mix.

A few fae clock me, I guess I stand out with my brightly coloured hair, but it seems as though the novelty of seeing humans—who really look just like fae but with rounded ears—has worn off.

I haven't been able to smoke any herbs today, and I dare not eat anymore golden cap, so I'm feeling a bit anxious around others. Even back at the palace I suspect I would run into Charlotte, Edith, or the High Lord, even if I holed up in my room. So, I decided to seek out solace in order to be able to think clearly.

I break free from the buildings and step out onto the promenade, the sun beaming down on me as if happy to see me. It's quieter on the beach today, and I wonder if preparations are being made to host the High Lord of Autumn Court and his new mate.

Just the thought sets my stomach flipping. Seki has agreed to stay in Ethea, she has accepted a mating bond. I'm glad that she's happy, but it puts me in a strange position. If both of us had rejected the bond, perhaps I wouldn't feel so…guilty. Like I'm doing the wrong thing. But knowing that Seki has accepted it, and is staying…

I stomp along the beach, kicking up sand in my haste and reach the end of the bay in no time. The beach beyond the outcropping is empty, but I'm still not *alone* enough. I discard my flip flops, my bag, and my dress, tucking them high up on a natural shelf, then turn and head into the waves.

A sigh escapes me as I wade deeper into the water. I'm waist high before I know it and waste no time launching myself out into the bay, swimming towards Turtle Rock with easy yet urgent strokes.

By the time I reach the waterfall my muscles are pleasantly aching. I pause outside the cave and look up at the cliffs, I hadn't looked at them properly the last time I was here. They are white, like the homes in the city, and I imagine them to be soft like chalk, but they look more durable, less… crumbly.

I paddle closer to the fall itself, enjoying the sound of water rushing down the cliff face. It's like white noise, drowning out my frenzied thoughts. Slowly, I swim under the cascade of water, closing my eyes and letting it pelt the top of my head and shoulders. The sensation steals away my breath and I push past with a gasp.

Once inside I open my eyes again, and the cave is just as magical as I remember. The openings overhead let in glittering beams of light and small amounts of foliage creep through the cracks. The air is thick with spray from the waterfall, and it catches the streaks of sunlight, creating a canopy of rainbows.

To my right is the rock ledge that the High Lord laid

me out on. My core tightens at the thought of him between my legs and I press my thighs together until the ache subsides because that isn't helping. Yeah, I can't sit up there.

I swim past the ledge to the crescent of sand at the back and wade out of the water, finding myself a nice smooth rock to sit on instead. Despite the moisture in the air, and being underground, its surprisingly mild in here. I look around again, admiring my surroundings and shouldn't be shocked that another wave of belonging washes over me. I can't help but think if I stayed in Summer Court, I could come here to clear my head anytime I liked.

If I stayed in Summer Court, I could swim in the ocean every day. I could explore the coastline and discover other caves or remain on the beach and sunbathe. I could gorge myself on olives, figs, and those delicious honey cakes that were served at dinner last night. My exploration of the cliffs didn't exactly go to plan, I could walk along those coast paths for miles and miles, watching the ocean stretch out endlessly. If that got boring, there is plenty more to see; the High Lord said there were deserts and mountains, forests, and meadows…

If I stayed, I would be with *him.* I could kiss him as often as I liked. I imagine lazy mornings in bed, the sun streaming in from the window, painting the room gold as we touched and pleasured one another. The room echoes with moans and gasps, and I feel the soft caress of his feathered wings. The thought fills me with a different kind of happiness, an echo of something I can't quite put my finger on, and the bond seems to pulse inside me.

But if I stayed… there are things I could never do, never achieve. I still haven't been to the Great Wall in China or seen the fjords in Norway. I've never skydived from a plane or swum with sharks. A hundred different experiences race through my head, things I have had on my 'to do list.' Like visit an elephant sanctuary in Thailand, be in Mexico for Día de los Muertos, or taste authentic biryani in India.

I sigh, wrapping my arms around my legs and rest my head on my knees. Why can't I wrestle my thoughts into some sort of order? Why can't I make a decision? Why does going to Spring Court feel like I'm running away?

Because the bond is affecting your thoughts, I think to myself unhelpfully. That's the problem. I don't know what's real and what's the bond. Would I even be considering staying if it weren't for the magnetic pull I feel towards the High Lord? (I don't even know his *name*!) Would I feel so 'at home' here if it weren't for the fae magic messing with me?

I close my eyes and huff out a frustrated breath. Why is this so hard? I listen to the waterfall again, and the gentle splash of waves against rocks, letting the sound soothe my thoughts. Thick, salty air fills my lungs even as the sand tickles my toes.

I'm staying here until I decide, I vow…I might be here a while.

Chapter 21

High Lord

I groan as cold salty water splashes against my heated skin. The day is no warmer than any other, and yet frustration boils through me. At first, I thought it was simply my need for my mate. When I woke this morning, my cock was achingly hard, and I irritably stroked it to release. But it did nothing.

The palace then seemed suffocating; humid and oppressive. My bond to Willow burning within me, unsatisfied. And so, I made my way down to the beach, eager for solitude, and to feel the chill of the waves against my skin.

The cool waters of Summer Bay ease the ache a little as I swim out of my depth. As far as I can see aquamarine waters glitter under the sun, interrupted only by Turtle Rock. When I reach the uniquely shaped stone, I turn back to face my court.

Even this far away my court is magnificent. The white and blue buildings shine like gems amidst the sand. The pale blue sky stretches overhead, dotted with only a handful of puffy white clouds. And then there are the high cliffs that encircle the bay, topped with tall, proud cypress trees. It is beautiful. I am biased perhaps, but I cannot believe anyone would want to leave this place.

I sigh and continue swimming, heading for my cave. The cascading sound of the waterfall is comforting to me, and I pause beneath it, willing the torrent of water to wash away my despair.

After a moment I paddle forward and breath deep, the uniquely salty scented air of the cave filling my lungs. I open my eyes and let them adjust to the glittering colourful light streaking in from above.

When my gaze lowers and I look around my secret haven I spot another, sat on the small stretch of sand at the back. I know in an instant that it is Willow. Not from her golden skin, or the damp blue curls that caress her shoulders, but from the way my heart begins to thump wildly at the sight of her, and the bond in my chest tightens, as if drawing me closer to my mate.

I should leave, turn, and swim back, giving her space and peace, but surely this is the fates design, that we should both be here at the same time. I paddle a little closer before announcing my presence.

"Willow," I call out, my voice echoing off the cave walls.

Her head snaps up from its previous position resting on her knees and her expression turns to worry.

"I'm sorry," she apologises when I am close enough to hear her. "Should I not be here? Should I go?"

"No, do not be sorry, you may go where you wish," I explain. "May I join you?"

Some of the worry ebbs from her face as she nods, casting her eyes down as I wade out of the water. I am grateful, because the sight of her naked perched upon the rock is glorious, and as I move closer, I catch a glimpse of the pale thatch of hair between her legs. My cock instantly hardens and my mouth waters remembering her taste on my tongue. Perhaps this was a bad idea.

"I came here to think," Willow explains quietly as I wade out of the water and sit beside her. I position myself with my knee bent in an attempt to hide my erection.

"I did the same," I admit.

"Are you sure you don't mind me being here?"

A bitter laugh escapes my throat. "I don't mind. I enjoy your company."

"You do?"

She has to ask?

"Of course."

I see her nod out of the corner of my eye as silence falls between us. She still hugs her knees and watches the waves gently lap at the thin strip of sand in front of us.

"Are you considering going to Spring Court?" I ask, unable to help myself.

She doesn't answer right away, and I wonder if she heard me speak.

"I'm not sure. I thought about it, but…"

I hold my breath. Is she considering staying? When she doesn't continue, I encourage her gently.

"But?"

She glances at me, her mesmerising features contorted with apprehension. I long to reach out and caress her, comfort her, if only to let her know that she can speak her mind freely with me. Even if she thinks I do not wish to hear what she has to say. I would rather know her thoughts. She looks away again, resting her chin on her knees.

"I'm so confused," she sighs. "I love it here, your court is beautiful, and I feel like I…like I could *belong* here, but that's just the bond tricking me, right?"

"I don't think so—"

"And then there's you. You have been good to me, and when I'm around you I feel… it doesn't matter what

I feel because its fake. It's all just magic messing with my emotions."

"I don't think the bond works like that Willow. The fates create the bond to bring two people together, I don't think their magic effects emotions. Heightens them perhaps, but it doesn't create something from nothing."

She turns to me again, her silver eyes watering. When she frowns, I cannot look away. What I would give to caress her, to comfort her.

Delicate fingers brush my skin as she rests her hand on top of mine and squeezes my fingers.

"I was harsh with you the last time we were here. Not wanting a mate has nothing to do with you personally, it's just that I… I don't think I'm cut out to be your mate—anyone's mate."

"Because you would feel trapped?" I ask her.

"Yeah," she nods. "I keep thinking about what I would lose if I stayed—all the things I would miss. But then I think about being here—about Summer Court, about you…"

I stay silent waiting for her to continue, but she does not. Instead, she looks down at our joined hands and gently rubs my fingers with her thumb. My heart aches with need for her and I long to touch her, kiss her, but the air between us feels too fragile.

"I understand," I tell her.

"You do?"

I nod. "When I was young, I was frivolous with my magic, and I would fly all the time. I have watched the sunrise from hundreds of feet above the bay, I have played in the rain, wrestled with the wind, and danced in the clouds. Now I can barely summon my wings and am all but bound to the ground. I often feel…contained, trapped. I think that is similar to the feeling you fear."

Willow watches me carefully, a spark of pity in her eyes.

"I do not wish for you to feel that way," I tell her, and I cannot help myself; I reach out and brush my fingers against her cheek. "All I want is your happiness."

"Even if that means that I leave?"

I do my best not to grimace at her words. "Yes," I choke out.

She reaches for me then, her palm pressing softly to my jaw. Her fingers tighten around mine, our hands still joined between us. The silver of her eyes shimmers as she leans towards me, pale lashes fluttering closed. Warm lips brush against mine and my breath catches in my lungs. I lean into her, pressing my mouth to hers as my fingers slide to the nape of her neck, tangling in her wavy tresses.

Her lips part on a sigh and her tongue darts out seeking mine. I meet her eagerly, caressing hers with my own in a hot, devouring kiss. Her lips taste salty, but her mouth, her tongue, is all Willow, sweet and earthy all at once and I am lost.

I pull her towards me, closing the gap between us, desperate for her touch, as a drowning man is desperate for air. Releasing her hand, I wrap an arm around her waist, holding her against me. Her free arm curls around my side, her palm pressed across my back. A soft moan escapes her, and I devour it, drunk on the sound.

"Wait," she breathes, pulling away. "I can't do this," she tells me, her voice strained.

Willow leans forward again, resting her head against my chest, her hands still at the nape of my neck and across my back. I hold her close, both arms wrapped around her.

"Can't do what?" I ask, though I am terrified of the answer.

"I can't be who you want me to be," she explains. "I'm sorry."

"I understand," I tell her, though it kills me, as I

stroke up and down her back. "I understand," I repeat, resting my head atop hers.

"I think I should go to Spring Court."

I cannot speak, my worst fear confirmed forms a knot in my throat. Right now, my mate is in my arms, soft and delicate. Her skin is a pale warm gold against my dark cold brown and I would give anything to remain this way for eternity. But the decision is not mine.

"If you must," I manage eventually.

When she pulls away, I let her, though every muscle in my body screams in protest to hold her tighter. She looks up at me, her expression reflecting the sorrow I feel.

"I must," she nods. "I can't think straight when I'm here. When I'm with you, my thoughts get all jumbled and all I want to do is kiss you and… I need space… I need to be *away* from you, from Summer Court. Maybe then I'll be able to think clearer… maybe…"

"The choice is yours Willow, I will not stop you if you wish to leave."

"Thank you," she whispers.

I manage a weak smile, even though inside I feel as if I'm dying. The fates are cruel, to choose me a mate who does not want me. A female so perfect I would give my life for hers, and yet it is not to be.

Just as a bird does not belong in a cage, and a fish does not belong in a tank, Willow does not deserve to be tethered to me, to my court. Her free spirit and desire for adventure is part of who she is, I could never douse that fire in her. I want Willow just as she is. But she does not want me.

"Will you swim back with me?" She asks. It is a peace offering. She knows her decision has struck me deep, but it cannot be any other way. She has to choose her freedom above all else and I respect that.

"Of course."

Chapter 22

Willow

I haven't seen the High Lord for three days. Not since I told him I was going to go to Spring Court, not since we kissed. I miss him.

Is he avoiding me? Or am I subconsciously avoiding him? Admittedly I have been going to the dining hall either early or late. But whenever I go, he is not there, nor has he been from what I can tell.

Going to Spring Court is the right thing to do. It will give me space to think. Maybe once I'm there, without the distraction of *him,* I will be able to get my thoughts in order. I'll be free of the magnetic pull I feel towards him (hopefully) and able to stop thinking about him. About how he risked his life to save me, how good and right his arms and wings felt around me. How much I enjoy kissing him, and how I can't stop thinking about… *more.*

A knock at my door pulls me from my thoughts. I get up from my perch on the bed, where I was adding more notes to my journal (maybe daydreaming about the High Lord) and plod over to open it.

My heart skips a beat when I swing the door open and reveal *him*, as if he had been summoned by my thoughts. Today he is dressed in a sort of toga. Creamy gold fabric drapes over one broad shoulder, revealing a slither of his toned chest and accentuating his muscular arms. The fabric gathers at his hips and forms a pleated skirt. Half his locs have been gathered at the top of his head in a knot, leaving the rest to cascade down his back. At his neck hangs an ornate golden sun medallion which matches the fastenings on his toga and the thin leather straps of his sandals which crisscross up his thick calves.

He looks divine. Like some sort of Greek god, and my mouth waters at the sight.

"Good morning, Willow," he greets me, the deep rumble of his voice sending a shudder all the way through me.

"Good morning," I reply, my voice sounding a little flustered.

"May I come in?"

"Sure."

I step aside to allow him past, then close the door. He stands in the middle of the room, the pose would look awkward on anyone else, yet he looks statuesque.

"I won't take up too much of your time, I just… I wanted to give you a small gift."

"A gift?"

He nods and reaches into his pocket. When his hand withdraws, he's holding a single white feather the length of my forearm. As he hands it to me it catches the sunlight coming in from the balcony and shimmers with a golden lustre.

"From your wing?"

"It is. I saw that you had collected some of the oak leaves of Autumn Court for your journal, I thought this would make a pleasant addition. Something to remember me by."

"You plucked out one of your wing—"

He chuckles and shakes his head. "No, my wings were not harmed in the process, occasionally the feathers fall out naturally."

I reach out and take the feather, my fingers brush his and just that minute touch sends a tingle down my arm. *Get it together, Willow.*

I hold the feather in my hand carefully, smoothing over the silky whisps.

"It's beautiful," I say, more to myself than him, as I remember how I had stroked his wings the night he saved me. This single feather is just as soft as I recall the others being and it fills me with a strange sense of sadness.

"I have nothing to give you in return."

"You needn't give me anything."

I frown at his answer and head over to my bed, gently tucking the feather between the pages of my journal. When I turn back to the High Lord, he is watching me carefully. There is a smile on his lips, but it doesn't reach his eyes. The mesmerising golden brown churns with sorrow instead and makes my chest ache because I know I am the cause. Is this why he has kept his distance the last few days?

I glance away, awkwardly smoothing out the folds of my coral pink dress, my bangles jangling at the movement. It gives me an idea. Closing the distance between us, I stride across the room to the High Lord.

"Here," I say as I pull one of the bangles from my wrist. "It isn't much, but…"

His smile widens, a hint of it reaching his eyes as he holds out his hand to accept my gift. His fingers caress the underside of my hand as he takes the bracelet, and my pulse stutters.

"It's the same colour as your hair," he observes, twirling it in his fingers before sliding it over his fist. The bangles are loose on my thin wrists, but it looks a little tight on his and the sight makes me giggle.

"Thank you, Willow, I shall wear it always."

When I look up at him—because he is a good foot taller than me—my laugh dies in my throat. The sadness has returned to his eyes, and it breaks my heart. I feel awful that I am the cause. I want to tell him I'll stay, if only to see him smile again, but that wouldn't be fair. It has crossed my mind a hundred times, a thousand, in the last few days that I could. I could stay here, with him, try and give the mates thing a go, but the thought still scares me. I'd be giving up my freedom, based on feelings that have been put there by magic. What if they fade? What if agree to be his mate and the spell is broken and I feel nothing for him, I will be stuck here. Yet seeing him so crestfallen fills me with an urgent need to comfort him—

The door to my room flies open as Charlotte bursts through it.

"They're here!" She cries excitedly, then freezes when she sees us. "Oh… sorry."

"It's quite alright," the High Lord answers, all formality. "Thank you, Charlotte, I should make my way to the throne room." With that he bows his head to us both, then promptly leaves the room. I sigh, feeling oddly lonely in his absence.

"Sorry," Char says again, "Were you two having a moment?"

I huff a laugh. "Yeah, I guess we kind of were."

"I didn't mean to interrupt."

"I know, it's fine. You probably stopped me doing something silly anyway," I sigh, crossing the room to my friend.

"You look stunning by the way," I remark, admiring her new dress. She's a vision in the shimmering pearlescent pink which reminds me of the inside of a shell. Combined with the pink streaks in her hair she looks like raspberry ripple ice cream.

She blushes and smiles, her gaze dropping to the floor. I take her by the arm, linking mine with hers and head out into the hallway.

"Are you sure you want to come to Spring Court with the rest of us?" She asks after a few moments.

"I think so."

"Well, that doesn't sound very convincing."

"I guess not," I chuckle. "What else can I do? When I'm around him my thoughts go to mush. I need time away, space to figure out what I'm going to do. Consider my options."

"That sounds like you're *considering* staying."

"I'm considering *all* my options." I explain. And I am. She doesn't need to know that I am considering some more than others.

We are the last two to arrive. The High Lord already sits on his throne, a golden circlet now across his brow and his magnificent wings stretched out behind him. I feel a stab of pity, knowing what it costs him simply to have them on display. But he looks resplendent up there in all his glory, so much so it makes my knees weak. I look away quickly before I stumble.

To his right stands his grumpy twin, who is wearing some sort of golden armour on his chest emblazoned with the same sun symbols that was on the High Lord's necklace. The emblem of their court perhaps? Next to him stands the High Lady of Autumn, dressed in her Autumn Court finery.

To the High Lord's left stands K, an excitable grin on his face. He's wearing an aquamarine tunic embroidered with the sun (definitely the court emblem) which compliments his cool brown skin. Beside him stands the rest of the humans, so Charlotte and I shuffle across the hall and join them.

Others have gathered in the hall; nobles and courtiers I assume, and two rows of well presented, emblem bearing guards create a walkway down the center of the room. Clearly Summer Court puts on a finer welcome for the High Lord of a neighbouring court than it does for other High Fae.

The columned white marble room has also been decorated with blue and gold banners, all bearing the sun of the Summer Court. I can't help but smile with a strange sense of… pride?

Trumpets blare, filling the hall with their celebratory sound, announcing the arrivals. The High Lord of Autumn enters first looking very fancy in high waisted trousers, a billowing shirt with a waist coat and *cloak.* It's a bit hot for all that, but I assume its formal Autumn Court livery, especially as it's emblazoned with oak leaves. Beside him Seki looks stunning, her pumpkin orange dress flowing around her as she glides alongside her High Lord.

Her mate.

She's practically glowing, a beaming smile on her face, as she slides her hand into the High Lord's, and they share an adorable glance of affection at one another. That's when I notice her ears, they poke out of her onyx hair, now elongated. "She's fae." I hear someone gasp.

Behind them enters Amber and Riley. I can't help but smile at the sight of them. Amber looks as classy and elegant as ever, if a little tired, while Riley looks adorable in a waist coat and bow tie. I've missed those two.

When they reach the dais they halt, the small contingent of guards behind them rattling in their armour as they follow suit. Greetings and pleasantries are exchanged, then the guards are dismissed. Seki tiptoes, kissing her High Lord on the cheek before gliding over to us, Riley, and Amber in tow.

I pull Seki in for a hug when she reaches me. She giggles then obliges, hugging me back. So ensues a series of hugs, including Mollie, until the 'Summer Court humans' have each hugged the 'Autumn Court humans'…and Seki, I guess, now she's fae.

When the initial excited chatter starts to die down, I notice Seki's expression turn a little solemn. She tucks her hair behind one pointed ear and glances around the group awkwardly.

"I guess we need to talk."

Chapter 23

High Lord

"So, tell me of your mate," I prompt as I offer the High Lord of Autumn a glass of wine.

"My thanks."

He takes a slow sip, humming his approval, as I sit on the chaise opposite him. I hide my eagerness to hear how he convinced his mate to stay by picking an olive from the bowl beside me and popping it into my mouth.

"I knew the moment I saw her," the High Lord begins, his grin all male pride. "In truth, I nearly fell from my horse, so forcefully did the bond snap. In the beginning I said nothing of it. They were all angry or scared…some both, and I didn't want to frighten her away. I thought with time she might come to appreciate my court and I would have the chance to explain once she was more settled. But the fates it would seem had other plans." He takes another sip of wine and I ignore the gurgling impatience in my stomach.

"Seki and some of her friends were spending a lot of time in my library and stumbled upon a text that explained the mating bond, in part at least. She was angry that I had concealed the information from her, I thought I lost her then. That was when I received word from Nandra that Winter had attacked, and I had to leave my court."

"I hope all is well there," I interject.

"Thank you, it is. But we will need to discuss Winter."

I nod my agreement, plucking another olive from the bowl, and wait for him to continue telling me of his mate.

"By the time I returned to my court, Seki had calmed down, and thought on the situation. She asked many questions—I am sure you are aware by now, that the humans exchange questions easily."

Again, I nod.

"I answered them all and waited patiently. After a few days she accepted the bond," he smiles to himself.

"Truly I am the most blessed of fae, my Seki is… perfect."

"I am pleased for you," I congratulate tightly, trying to keep the envy from my voice.

His mate accepted the bond, where mine has not. I will never know the happiness he does, and while I do not begrudge him, we are neighbours, friends even, he has that which I long for with all my being.

"I wondered if perhaps you had found a mate among the humans," he speculates, and I laugh darkly at his accuracy.

"I have," I admit. "Willow is my mate, but she…she has an adventurous spirit, and has rejected the bond."

"My sympathies then. I would not wish that on an enemy, let alone a friend." His voice is thick with sincerity.

"I had thought to seek advice from you," I confess. "The decision to stay or leave is hers of course, but I wonder if there is something I might yet do to…" I cannot find the word. Persuade? Encourage? They do not sit right on my tongue. I do not wish to force her decision, but I would do anything to prove myself a worthy mate. Not wishing to appear weak or desperate in front of another High Lord though, I keep my thoughts to myself.

"Trust the Fates. My Seki is speaking with the humans even now, she is happy with our mating. Perhaps her happiness will sway your mate's decision."

I bob my head considering his words. Though I know nothing of Seki, I do wonder if the account of a human who has accepted the bond will affect Willow's decision. Hope flares, rattling the bond and I feel it grow a little brighter. I dare not cling to it too hard though, it feels like water cupped in my hands, more likely to spill through the gaps and vanish, than remain in my possession. I must accept that my mate may yet chose to leave.

"Thank you. Your words are reassuring."

"I hope that Willow chooses to stay. I wish for the happiness of being mated for you, my friend."

I smile and nod at him. The thought of us both being mated is a joyous one. We are close Autumn and Summer, closer than any other two courts. His sister after all, the Lady of Autumn, was born of a Summer Court female. It would bring us closer together still if both of our mates were friends.

"My thanks." There is nothing left to say on the matter. Willow will make her decision and I will accept it whatever it is. There is nothing more I can do but wait. It is as if I have a spear aimed at my heart poised to strike.

I push my anxiety aside, as there are other matters that need to be addressed.

"Now, let us discuss what we are going to do about Winter Court."

Chapter 24

Willow

"What do you think she will do?" I ask Seki when she finishes telling me about Yasmin's situation.

"I don't know. It's her decision either way. I've told her the same as I've told you and the others; Everything about magic, the bond and how it works. I think it's important to know all the details before deciding, and I know from experience how difficult it can be to find that out from *them,"* she chuckles.

From the sounds of it, it took her mate a lot longer to come to terms with the whole 'questions' thing than it did the Summer Court fae. K and the High Lord seem to have picked it up quite quickly… I'm not sure about the High Lords twin though… I haven't actually heard him speak since that argument with Mollie.

I look at Seki, the way her skin glows, the elegant point of her ears, the way she wears the Autumn Court regalia proudly. She smiles a lot more now than she did when we first arrived in Ethea.

"You…you truly are happy?" I ask.

"I am," she nods, her smile widening.

"What was it like? When you accepted the bond?"

She thinks for a moment, fiddling with the beading

on her dress.

"It was like… everything fell into place. I knew I had made the right decision the moment I made it. Everything intensified as we spoke the words, my connection to the court, to him. It just felt … right, Like I had found where I truly belonged," she sighs dreamily. "Not to mention the sex is great!"

I'm so shocked by her candour that I burst into a fit of laughter and she follows. As we catch our breath, I consider her words. Especially the bit about 'finding where she truly belonged.' Haven't I been feeling like that since the moment I arrived here?

"I'm the High Lord of Summer's mate," I admit, my voice no more than a whisper.

"Oh! Congratulations!" Seki exclaims.

She must see the look on my face because her excitement disappears. "Not 'Congratulations'?"

"I don't know," I sigh. "I'm a traveller and adventurer, that's who I am. I can't *stay* here, cooped up in one place. I keep thinking about all the places I want to go to back in our realm, all the things I haven't done. I mean I haven't seen my parents in years, although I don't even know if they are alive. I mean they travel like me, so I'd probably never find them even if I tried.

"But then when I'm here it's like… I belong. I can't explain it, everything about Summer Court feels familiar. And then there's *him.* Seki, I can't stop thinking about him."

I tell her about everything that has happened; the bonfire and my spectacular vomiting, about the cave (which I give her directions to in case she wants to go there with her mate), the mushrooms, the shadows, and the way the High Lord held me when he saved me. Everything.

"Wow," Seki remarks, coming to sit beside me on the bed.

"I mean he said that if I stayed, I would be free to explore Ethea as much as I liked, but surely being his mate means I would have to stay here, he wouldn't want me galivanting off across the realm whenever I get wanderlust. And what if I see it all, what if I travel the whole realm and get bored, I won't be able to go home, I'd be stuck here! And—"

"Willow, Willow, breathe," Seki rests a hand on my leg to stop me in my ramble. "It's scary, I *know.* But let me tell you this; if he says you would be free to explore, he means it. The fae are honest—sure they might try to keep their secrets and avoid certain things, but when pushed they speak the truth.

"Also, I think you are focusing on all the things you would lose. We all have things we would miss from home. But in order to make an educated decision you should also consider what you will *gain.* A mate who will adore you, forever. You will also inherit his magic, from the wings and what you said about the day you took mushrooms, I'm assuming that his magic is flight. I think for someone who appreciates their freedom, that would be pretty awesome."

I nod, she's right, I have only focused on what I would lose.

"You would also become his High Lady; you would want for nothing. And your magic would help power his court, it would flourish once more. I know you can't base your decision on that alone, but I can tell you care about him. Seeing someone you care about get their full power, knowing that their court will thrive—that feels pretty damn good."

She's right. I think about what the High Lord told me about his flying, how he used to do it all the time, but now it's draining to merely summon his wings. I think about the closed down shops in the market, and the limited stock and produce in the remaining stalls and shops. If I stayed, I could help the court I feel at home in prosper.

"Ultimately," Seki continues. "It's your decision. I haven't regretted mine for a second, and I have never been happier. This is where I'm supposed to be, I really believe I was brought here by fate. But, at the end of the day, it's your choice, and if you want to leave, you won't be stopped."

"I know," I agree.

"Does that help?" She asks, and I nod my head.

"Yes, thank you Seki." She gives me a warm, genuine smile. "You remember what I told you?" I enquire with a playful wink, trying to change the subject.

"I do. In fact, I think I shall go find him now," she tells me, rising from the bed. "If you have any more questions…"

"I will ask. Thank you."

With one last nod, Seki leaves the room, and I am alone with my thoughts. She certainly gave me a fresh perspective: *Think about what you would gain.*

I'm reminded of my daydream; making love to the High Lord as the morning sun beams through the balcony window, a tangle of limbs and wings. I think about how easy it is to be around him, how I can't keep my hands to myself. How he makes me feel like a goddess. He risked his life to save me that night, and has promised me, more than once, that he would allow me every freedom.

The more I think about the positives, the more they start to outweigh the negatives. It's almost *too* good to be true; A handsome doting male, a rich land to explore to my heart's content and a court so beautiful it takes my breath away to call home.

Home.

Summer Court would be my home. The High Lord would be my home. No matter how far I ventured, no matter how long I chose to explore, I would always have somewhere to return to, *someone* to return to. The thought tightens in my throat, and my eyes water. Is that what I've been missing all along? Home for me has always been wherever I slept. I've never felt… connected to anywhere, always an outsider. Yes, I value my freedom, and the fact that I can just pack up and go whenever I choose, but I am always by myself. It's… kind of lonely. Even my parents had each other when they travelled, to share their adventures with.

If I stayed, I'd have a home, and I certainly wouldn't be alone anymore.

Seki was right. I started down this path of thought cautiously, taking each step carefully, but now I feel myself sprinting down it, because the further I go, the more *right* it feels.

A sob breaks free the moment I make my decision. But sadness is not the cause, it is relief, it is joy. I don't know how but I *know* I have made the right choice. I know what I must do. But first—I need to find my mate's brother.

Chapter 25

High Lord

The streets of Summer Court are empty as I guide the High Lord of Autumn down to the bay. His mate, Seki, walks beside him, her hand interlaced with his and my heart gives a pang of jealousy. They speak softly to one another, and I can't help but feel awkward.

The sound of drumming drifts along the cobbled streets towards us, filling the air with their beat and an orange glow tinges the deep blue sky, cast by the many bonfires that have been lit along the beach.

It is a pleasantly mild evening, very little breeze, and the air is still humid despite it being late autumn. I do not envy the High Lord beside me his formal regalia, tonight I am grateful for my traditional Summer Court robe.

We break free of the city and step out onto the promenade. I have never seen the beach so crowded. There are five bonfires each surrounded by fae, musicians and traders of all kinds mingling with the throng. I watch the two fae beside me as their faces light up with excitement. The High Lord bows to his High Lady, inviting her to dance and whisks her off towards the nearest fire.

Alone once more I pull my wings close and walk along the outskirts. I tell myself I'm not looking for Willow, but it is a lie. Every flash of blue I see draws my attention, and every time it is not her, I feel a stab of disappointment.

I find my twin first. He is hunched over, and as I draw closer; I notice he is talking to Mollie. I head towards them ready to intervene, but they are not arguing. That is unusual. I decide to leave them to it; she will be leaving for Spring Court with the others tomorrow no doubt. My brother will be happy about that, I'm sure.

Taking a drink as a server passes, I tip bright green liquid down my throat, enjoying the minty sensation on my tongue. I have no intention of getting drunk, neither do I plan to stay for long, but I am expected to show my face, to make an appearance. I only wish to see Willow once more enjoying my court before I must watch her leave in the morning.

My stomach clenches at the thought, like a knife to the gut. She did not seek me out after Seki spoke with her, so I assume her decision has not changed. Tomorrow my mate departs my court, and it is unlikely I will see her again. I reach for another drink, this one tart and citrusy, grapefruit I think, but it does nothing to dull my sorrow. I cannot linger here long.

Another flash of blue catches my attention and this time it is her. She is resplendent in a coral pink gown that accentuates the swell of her breasts and the sweep of her hips. Her azure hair cascades down her back in waves, and the bonfire makes her golden skin glisten. She is dancing with my younger brother and the two humans who arrived earlier, I cannot recall their names. I swear I can hear the sound of her bracelets jangling even over the roar of the bonfire and the pounding of drums.

I plan to simply admire her from afar, torture myself

just a little longer, but as if sensing my presence, she turns and spots me. A smile spreads across her lips before she says something quickly to the others then leaves them behind, hurrying over to me.

"There you are! I've been looking for you!" She greets excitedly, taking hold of my hands. "Come dance with me," she insists, dragging me towards the fire.

Who am I to deny her?

Once we are closer to the others she spins around, facing me, her arms reaching up to my shoulders and her fingers resting on the nape of my neck. Instinctively my hands go to her waist, holding onto her gently. I gaze down at her and force a smile, being this close to her, dancing with her, knowing she leaves tomorrow is the most acute torment. And yet I cannot pull away, every moment with her is precious. I breathe in her scent, warm and earthy, though not as earthy as usual—has she not smoked any herbs today? When she looks up at me, her silvery eyes are clear and bright—has she not drunk any alcohol either?

"This is where we first kissed," she says, a dreamy quality to her voice.

"It is."

"I'm sorry I ruined it by throwing up."

I can't help but chuckle. "Do not be sorry. It was perfect… up until you emptied your stomach onto the sand," I tease.

She smiles at me, and it is both pleasure and pain.

"You knew then, didn't you, that I was your mate?"

I sigh, leaning into my anguish. "Willow, I knew the moment you stepped into my throne room. My twin can tell you, I nearly stumbled down the dais."

When she giggles, it sends my heart stuttering, and I am aware all at once of her body pressed against mine as we sway to the beat of the drums. Her fingers stroke gently on the skin of my neck leaving a searing tingle in their wake.

Her gaze on me turns heated, and when her tongue darts out to dampen her lower lip, I am mesmerised. So much so I am late to notice her tip toeing. In the next moment, her mouth is against mine, her lips soft and warm. My grip on her hips tightens, as I run my tongue along her lower lip, seeking entry. She permits me, her tongue eagerly caressing my own. I lose myself in the taste of her, in the way she so fervently kisses me. She withdraws her tongue, her mouth closing and her lips lingering on mine for a moment before she pulls away. *No, no, that's not enough.*

"Come with me?" She asks, pressing a palm to my cheek, her expression pleading. All I can do is nod.

Willow takes my hand and leads me towards log seating where she scoops up her bag, which seems fuller than usual, then continues down the beach. She says nothing as she pulls me behind her and I realise that I would follow her anywhere, over the cliff edge if she demanded it.

We round the corner, onto the more private stretch of beach. In the distance I can see two fae laying naked in the sand and can just make out the sounds of their pleasure.

"Sit down a moment," Willow encourages me pointing to a rock.

I do as she asks, and the moment I am sat she sits across my thighs, her arms around my neck again and her bag resting on her lap.

"How would it work?" she questions. "If I were to stay."

If she were to stay? What new cruelty is this?

"What?" Is all I manage, what is she talking about?

"Say one morning I woke up, and I was full of wanderlust. You would simply let me leave, go where I liked?"

"I… yes," I breathe, my pulse quickening.

"And would you come with me?"

I swallow hard before answering. "I would come with you as often as my duties allowed, if that is what you wished."

"And if your duties prevented you from accompanying me, you would still let me go? Whenever and wherever, for as long as I wanted?"

"Of course. My only condition would be that you return to me every once in a while, because I… I would miss you fiercely."

She beams at me then, her hand coming to rest against my cheek. She dips her head and presses a gentle kiss to my lips then pulls away again before I can react.

"Are you taking the tonic—the one fae males take to prevent pregnancy?"

I frown at her question, and the sudden change in direction. What is going on?

"I am, but—"

"And do you have enough magic to fly us up to the cliffs, the spot where you found me the night I took the mushrooms?"

"I… I do, but, I would not have enough to fly us back," I tell her honestly.

Another smile.

"Don't worry about having enough to bring us back," she tells me.

"Why not?"

Her arms slide around my neck as she leans in close, her cheek against mine as she whispers in my ear.

"Because tonight, when I accept the bond, your magic will fulfil, and then you will be able to fly as often as you wish."

Chapter 26

Willow

I pull away to see his reaction. And chuckle when I see that it is both confused and full of hope.

"When…when you…"

"Mm hmm," I grin and nod, caressing his cheek.

"You… you're staying?" He chokes out.

"If you'll still have me?"

A ragged half laugh escapes him, and he beams at me. His breaths come quick and heavy as he searches my face, as if he still doesn't believe me.

"I'm staying," I confirm again, brushing another quick kiss to his lips.

"Say that again," he begs.

"I'm staying."

He laughs again, this time with joy and surprise. Clasping my cheeks, he pulls my mouth against his, devouring me with hot desperate kisses.

I pull away with a giggle. "I want to go up to the cliffs," I insist.

"Why?"

"I want you to claim me where you saved me. Please," I whisper the last word.

"Anything for you," he breathes, planting a quick kiss

to my cheek, before sliding an arm under my knees. He wraps the other around my waist and hauls me against his chest as he stands.

I cling to his shoulders as he launches us into the sky. A squeal of delight leaves me as I hold my mate tighter and squeeze my eyes shut. Wind rushes past me and whips at my hair to the steady beat of wings. The High Lord grips me tightly, holding me against his chest and I breathe him in; salt and sea breeze mixed with something else, something warm and comforting, like freshly baked bread.

There's a light jolt as we land, and I'm placed gently on the ground. But he doesn't let go, his hands rest on my arms as he gazes down at me in wonder. I can't help but beam at him. The gibbous moon overhead sets his onyx skin glowing, and the molten gold of his eyes steals away my breath. How did I ever think to leave him?

He looks away, studying our surroundings. "I'm not sure this will be comfortable—"

"I bought blankets!" I announce, setting my bag on the ground and pulling out the blankets K found for me, laying them out at my feet.

My mate chuckles, kissing me again. "Perfect," he whispers, and I'm not sure if he means the blankets or me.

I reach for him then, fumbling with the sun clasp on his shoulder. Finally, it releases and the fabric pools around his hips. The clasp of the skirt is easier and as the pleats fall away, he is left bare before me. My heart thumps in my chest, I am so full of need for him. I run my hands over his stomach, up to sculpted pectorals and along his broad shoulders. He shudders under my touch.

"Willow," he whispers, he hands coiling around my waist. Deft fingers undo the fastening of my dress, and it isn't long before it flutters to the floor. I gasp at the sensation, it isn't cold, far from it, and it's not as if I haven't been naked in front of him before but this is different.

I lower myself to the ground, and sprawl back across the blankets, patting the soft fabric beside me. My mate reaches for the gold band over his brow, pulling the circlet free and resting it upon a rock. He does the same with his medallion as my gaze wanders lower. He's already hard, his erection jutting out proudly from the vee of his hips and my pussy clenches at the sight.

He kneels, then stretches out beside me, adjusting his wings behind him, his hand wrapping around my waist pulling me close. When his mouth crashes against mine, his tongue darts out demanding entry. With a moan I open for him, welcoming him. His tongue surges forward, licking and caressing my own, his lips pressing against mine in an intoxicating bruising kiss.

A hand slides up my side to my shoulder, then back down to my hip, his touch scorching my skin. I'm vaguely aware of his cock pressing against my tummy as he continues to devour me and I'm panting already, shamelessly full of need, desperate of more.

I reach between us, stroking the head of his cock, which fits perfectly in my palm,

"Fates," he hisses as I grip him, twisting my fist over the already slick head.

As he peppers kisses along my jaw and below my ear, his hand glides lower, skimming over my thighs before dipping between my legs, caressing up the hot sensitive flesh of my inner thigh. I reach lower too, wrapping my fingers around his shaft, which is deliciously thick and veined, pumping him oh so gently.

He groans, nibbling on my ear lobe then licking up the column of my neck. His fingers reach the apex of my thighs, and he slowly runs a finger over the seam of my pussy, parting me. The sound my body makes as he drags his finger through my slick is delightfully obscene.

"So wet for me," he murmurs against my shoulder as his finger wanders higher to my clit, circling it gently.

I whimper at the torturous touch, my core clenching around nothing. Gripping him more firmly, I pump him harder. He groans, his fingers leaving my clit and sliding lower, teasing my entrance.

"Please," I beg, then cry out as he slips a finger into me. It feels so good, and yet it's not enough.

My other hand slides over his shoulder, up the back of his neck and I grip a handful of his locs, pulling him back to kiss me again. He chuckles as I devour him, desperately kissing him, my hips rocking against his hand of their own accord.

Another finger joins the first, dipping in and out of me in a gloriously tortuous rhythm. I'm keening, rolling my hips trying to get more friction. Impatiently I shift, sliding myself under him, encouraging him on top of me. He obliges, shifting his own weight so he rests on one arm, his big body covering mine, his wings draped either side of us, shimmering in the moonlight.

I let go of his cock, both hands sliding over his back, mindful of the delicate feathers where his wings meet his shoulder blades. My fingers glide over soft skin pulled taught over hard muscle that ripples under my touch. His fingers slide out of me, and he brings his hand up between us. I drag my teeth over my lower lip as he puts both fingers in his mouth and sucks them clean.

"You taste like paradise," he tells me, voice deep and gravely. My whole-body quivers at the decadent sound.

He shifts over me again, his heated expression turning to something more tender. Fingers gently caress my cheek.

"Are you sure this is what you want?" He asks, voice dripping with restraint and desire.

I wrap my arms around him tightly, bending my

knees and caressing the back of his calves with my feet.

"I'm sure," I breathe, lifting my knees higher, wrapping my legs around his hips, and locking my feet together.

"You know the words?"

"Yes, Seki told me," I confirm, squeezing my thighs impatiently.

He nods, and a few of his locs fall forward, tickling the side of my face and neck. Reaching between us, he rubs the head of his cock along my seam, coating himself in my wetness. I moan, clenching around air again. The need to be filled pulses through me, I need him so badly.

"*Please,*" I whimper.

After another swipe up and down he positions himself at my entrance. His gaze lifts to me, his eyes full of hunger, even as his palm comes to rest on my cheek.

"Ready?" He asks and all I can do is nod, my body aching and desperate.

He eases into me a fraction and I gasp.

"I Vias, High Lord of Summer Court," he grits out, as he feeds another inch into me. "Claim you Willow as my mate."

I moan as he sinks deeper. "I Willow, of the human realm," Vias groans as he presses into me, my body stretching in the most glorious way to accommodate him. "Accept you Vias, as my mate."

A guttural cry tears from my throat as he surges all the way into me, filling me.

"Willow," he growls. "My Willow, my mate."

He pulls out, almost fully before plunging in again, pumping into me in hard slow strokes.

My orgasm is already building as Vias dips his head, his mouth crashing into mine, devouring me in a searing, claiming kiss. I am nothing but light, as the bond flares through me, shinning like the sun as it breaches the horizon at daybreak.

I cling to Vias as my body tightens. One hand grips a palmful of his locs, the other claws at his back as I grind my hips up to meet his trusts. My head falls back as my orgasm barrels through me. It explodes, like fireworks, leaving flashing lights dancing behind my eyes. I scream my pleasure for the whole realm to hear.

Vias continues to pound into me, as the ripples of my orgasm start to recede, still chasing his own. My back twitches, the muscles in my shoulders contorting uncomfortably. The realisation is blurry in my post-orgasm haze, but I know I don't want to be laying on my back when it happens. I push my mate, flipping him onto his back and straddling his hips. He shuffles under me, finding a more comfortable position as his wings splay out beneath him.

Hands resting on his hard sculpted stomach I rock my hips, riding him with abandon. In this position his cock feels even deeper. I'm keening and panting again already. Vias grips my hips as he thrusts his up to meet me, his gaze fixed on where our bodies join.

I groan as my back spasms, writhing on top of my mate, but that only adds to the friction between my legs, and I groan again for an entirely different reason. Still gripping my hips, Vias' hand splays, allowing his thumb to slip between my folds and graze over my clit.

"Vias!" I moan, as he circles the sensitive bud and everything clenches. The muscles in my shoulders convulse as my orgasm builds and I'm caught between pleasure and pain.

"*Fates,*" Vias grunts, his hips jerking beneath me as he finds release, just as my own orgasm rips through me. I buckle forward with a cry, squeezing my eyes shut as I come.

At the same moment, my wings erupt behind me, unfurling into the night. The weight of them surprises me and I sink down to lay across Vias' chest, still gasping for air. His hands rest gently on my lower back as I listen to his heart thumping against my ear in unison with my own.

After a moment, once my breathing has slowed, and my body has stopped trembling, I sit up. I roll my shoulders, trying to find a comfortable way to manage the weight of my wings.

"They're so heavy," I complain.

Vias chuckles in response, his body jolting and I whimper when I realise he's still inside me. The movement sends tingles all over my skin and makes my pussy clench.

Nope, I need a minute.

I shift my weight, lifting myself from Vias' still throbbing cock and kneel at his side. He props himself up on his elbows and watches me carefully. His body glistens with sweat and his locs which have come loose of their knot now cascade around his handsome face. There's a haze in his eyes and his lips look a little swollen from all our frantic kissing. *Damn, he's gorgeous.*

"Are you well my mate?" He asks.

"Yeah, I just…" I roll my shoulders again, my wings tugging uncomfortably. "How do I get rid of them?"

"Get rid of them?" Vias chuckles, an eyebrow raised.

"Yeah, you know, make them disappear like you do."

He laughs again—the sound going straight to my clit—before answering. "Don't think of it as *getting rid* of them, they are sacred after all. Instead, imagine pulling them close, drawing them into yourself."

I do as he suggests, pulling at my wings rather than pushing them. I flex my back a few times before the weight lightens. After another roll of my shoulders and a deep breath the feathers of my wings give a gentle rustle then curl in on themselves and vanish.

"Oh, that's better," I sigh, laying down beside Vias.

He pulls me close, wrapping an arm around my shoulders, and resting his large palm on my hip.

"You'll get used to it," he reassures me, pressing a tender kiss to my forehead.

I snuggle closer, resting my head on his chest and draping an arm over his hips. I don't care that he's all sweaty, I'm not exactly fresh as a daisy.

"How do you feel?" He asks, his finger stroking my shoulder.

"Like I've run a marathon."

"A marathon?"

"It's a long race humans compete in."

"Ah."

My back doesn't hurt as much now, it just aches like everything else. I shuffle a little, trying to get more comfortable and cringe when I feel how my hair has stuck to my clammy skin. I reach up to peel it away, tucking a few curls behind my ear.

My ear.

I run my fingers up the out edge, feeling along the now elongated point. The higher I touch, the more sensitive it feels, and my body gives a gentle shudder of pleasure. *Interesting.*

Vias runs his hand along my waist, drawing my attention. "Any regrets?" he asks softly.

I prop myself up on my elbow so I can look at my mate properly. The haze has faded from his eyes, and now he watches me with concern. Did he really think I would regret accepting the bond? I place my palm against his face and rub his cheek with my thumb, leaning forward to gently brush my lips to his.

"None," I tell him, and kiss him again.

I am rewarded with a grin, his golden eyes glittering. "What made you change your mind?"

I consider my answer a moment, reaching for one of

his locs. It's about the thickness of a pencil and I enjoy the felt like texture as I twirl it around my finger.

"It was lots of little things I suppose but when I spoke to Seki earlier, the last few things fell into place."

"Such as?"

I tilt my head before running a finger along Vias' strong brow, down his nose, then trace his lips. I can't stop touching him, I've been holding back for so long. Luckily, he doesn't seem to mind.

"Such as feeling at home here the moment I arrived, the feeling of 'rightness' and 'belonging, not just in Summer Court, but with you, not to mention how amazing you have been." He grins at me proudly.

"She also told me about the deal with your magic, how it would fulfil when we accepted the bond—oh Vias your magic!"

I sit up, excitement pulsing through me. "Do you want to go flying?"

"I think you need a few lessons first my mate," Vias advises, sitting up and smoothing the back of his hand down my arm.

"Not with me," I insist. "You should go on your own."

My suggestion is met with a furrowed brow.

"You have been grounded for so long, I know what it means to you to have your full magic… you shouldn't have to wait. I want your first flight to be unencumbered." I press my palm to his chest, right over his heart, and notice him glance up at the sky before retuning his gaze to me.

"You wouldn't mind?"

"Not in the slightest," I reassure him. "Go, be *free*. Fly as long as you like, I'll wait right here. I'm not going anywhere."

He beams at me, taking my face in his hands and pressing a deep kiss to my lips.

"Thank you, Willow. Truly, I am the most blessed of fae." He stands, one palm still cupping my cheek. "You're sure—"

"Go."

With a nod he turns, facing the horizon, the waves below the cliffs glittering in the moonlight. He charges for the edge then without hesitation dives off the cliff. I gasp, feeling a brief moment of panic. But in the next breath he surges back into view soaring upwards with a triumphant bellow.

My heart swells at his joy, my eyes watering. Then I giggle to myself when I realise he is flying over his court naked. He's so high up though, I doubt anyone can see him in all his glory.

I roll one of the blankets up, creating a makeshift pillow, then lay back and watch him. My mate glides and swoops across the starry sky, his movements fluid and elegant. He loops in front of the moon, then dives again, only to soar back up a moment later.

I can't stop smiling.

My eyes start to feel heavy, and I shuffle down the blanket to get more comfortable. I stretch my muscles, which are aching in the best possible way then let my eyes flutter shut. A hum escapes me as I wallow in contentment—no not contentment, this is not short lived or fleeting. What I feel is happiness, and I know, with absolute certainty that it will be long lasting and enduring.

I sigh listening to the gentle roll of the waves in the bay and I swear I can hear the distant beat of my mate's wings. Then, with a smile on my face, I drift off to into a deep, peaceful sleep.

Chapter 27

Vias

I wake with my mate in my arms.

A surge of joy rushes through me, as I hold her close, her slight body tucked perfectly against mine, her back to my chest, as if she belongs there. She *does* belong there I remind myself with a grin.

Her head rests on my arm, even as it curls around her, my other is resting on the curve of her hip. Unable to help myself, I lean closer, nestling my nose into her turquoise curls and breathe in her scent, warm and earthy.

I release a sigh as my morning erection twitches and tighten my hold on her. She is mine. She accepted the bond, and I will wake every morning with this incredible female in my arms. Well, almost every morning. Maybe not when she is off exploring, but even that doesn't bother me so much. I will miss her for certain, but her absence will only make our reunions all the sweeter, and I will greatly enjoy listening to her tales of adventure.

Willow sleeps on and I dare not move through fear of waking her, even though my muscles strain to be stretched. I ache all over, from our lovemaking and my flight after. I do not know how long I flew for, as I was lost in the sheer joy of flying freely, with no concern over how much magic I expended. Not only did my mate accept the bond last night, a gift in itself, but she gave me back my wings, my ability to fly and all the pleasure that encompasses.

I had returned from my flight to find Willow curled up on the blankets, making adorable noises that let me know she was sleeping deeply. As I had laid down behind her and pulled her close, unable to resist holding her, she had mumbled incoherently, then settled once more. Shortly after I too had fallen asleep.

"Vias?" My mate asks softly, rousing.

"Here, my mate," I reassure her, stroking her hair away from her shoulder and giving it a gentle kiss. As I pull back, I see the two long silver streaks down her back, marking the location of her wings, at the inside curve of each shoulder blade. Interesting that hers are silver, where mine are gold. Not that they can usually been seen, as they are often hidden by my hair or clothing. But then I recall how the moonlight had shimmered off her when her wings unfurled for the first time as she rode my cock. She had looked magnificent, grinding herself on top of me, silvery white wings stretched behind her. My cock gives another twitch at the memory.

"Mmmm," Willow sighs, her fingers tracing up and down the veins in my forearm as she shifts backwards, pressing her backside against my groin.

I kiss her shoulder again, as my hand caresses the curve of her waist. A soft moan escapes her, and she rolls her hips again, the pressure against my already hard cock delightfully torturous.

"Did my mate wake up wanting?" I ask, nuzzling her neck.

I feel her nod and slide my hand to her front, my fingers grazing the plains of her stomach. She writhes against me, her breath quickening as I kiss up the exposed column of her neck, then nip her ear. With the arm that's under her I reach for her breast, taking the small globe in my palm and massaging the flesh. My mate hums her approval as her hand reaches behind her, seeking my cock. Her fingers stroke up and down the underside with feather light touches before she grips my shaft more firmly.

With a groan against the curve of her neck I continue to kiss and lick her delicate skin, even as my hand slides lower, past her navel, brushing along the soft pale curls between her legs. Willow quivers, her grip on my cock faltering as I slide my finger down her seam, parting her gently. I groan again when I find her soaking, my fingers gliding easily through her wetness.

Rocking my hips, desperate for the friction of her fist around my length, I explore higher, seeking the bud at the top of her sex that drives her wild.

"Vias," she cries. Found it.

I circle the bundle of nerves with my finger leisurely, relishing the way my mate squirms at my touch. With my other hand I focus on her nipple, taking the hardened tip and rolling it between my thumb and finger, eliciting a moan from my mates lips.

She's panting now, grinding her backside against me, even as she pumps my cock.

"Willow," I whisper in her ear, my nose brushing the elongated edge, knowing how sensitive it is. "My beautiful mate, you look so lovely lost in your pleasure." I give her nipple a little pinch, as I apply more pressure with the fingers between her legs.

"Vias," she pants. "Please."

"What?" I growl. "Tell me what it is you want."

"This!" she moans, gripping my cock so hard its almost painful. I can't help the groan that escapes; I am a male possessed seeing my mate so desperate, her sex so slick and wanting, her scent perfuming the air, filling my lungs.

She whimpers as I lift my hand from my ministrations and take my cock from her. I adjust myself so that I can press the throbbing head to her entrance. She is dripping, so slick with desire that the need to claim her once more overcomes me with a fierceness like I have never felt before.

I sink into her welcoming heat with one fluid thrust, sheathing myself to the hilt. A guttural sound rips from her as her inner walls clench around me. *Fates, she feels so good.*

Lifting her leg over mine, I grip her hip and drive into her, enjoying the slippery sounds mixed with the slap of skin. Letting go of her hip, I slide my fingers once more between her folds, firmly circling her sensitive bud. She cries out, her palm fisting the blanket.

"Vias," she moans between ragged breaths.

"I love the sound of my name on your lips," I tell her, quickening my pace. My groin tightens and my muscles strain as I feel my release build. Not yet, my mate must have hers first.

"Vias! Oh God, Vi—"

Willow wails her pleasure, so loud that I wonder if my brothers can hear her. But I do not care. Her body pulses around my cock, gripping me tightly as I continue to pump into her. I pin her body to mine, so her smooth soft skin is pressed up against me and bury my head in her hair, sucking in her scent.

The bond between us thrums, as bright as the golden rays of the sun, blinding in its brilliance. My mate cries out again as she climaxes a second time, her entire body quaking in my arms. Once more, her body clasps the length of my cock and with one final thrust I am undone. My release roars through me as I am consumed with wave after wave of pleasure. I grit my teeth as every last drop of my spend is wrung from me, leaving me feeling dazed and lightheaded.

"*Fates,*" I hiss against Willow's shoulder as my cock twitches feebly.

Willow hums her satisfaction, her body limp in my arms. I skim my hand up and down her side affectionately as we both catch our breath. After a few moments, my mates grip on the blanket loosens and she wriggles away, detaching herself from me. She rolls towards me, draping her arm over my hip and snuggles close. I brush a few stray curls away from her brow, then rest my hand on her shoulders, drawing idle circles with my thumb.

"A girl could get used to starting the day that way," she says, beaming up at me. Her eyes are still hazy and there's a delightful flush to her cheeks.

"Anything you desire, my mate," I assure her, leaning in for a lazy kiss. Our lips meet and caress slowly, there is no urgency, only simple enjoyment. I sweep my tongue against hers one last time and give her bottom lip a teasing bite before pulling away.

"We should head back, the others will be leaving soon, and we need to be there to see them off."

Willow grumbles in response, burying her face against my chest in protest, making me chuckle.

"Once they have gone, I shall whisk you off to our chambers and we won't leave until you are entirely satisfied," I promise, kissing her brow.

"Mmmm, that sounds good," my mate sighs.

I hold her for a little longer, savouring the moment. It still doesn't feel real that this female is mine. A lifetime of moments like this stretch out in front of me and it fills me to the brim with joy. I kiss her brow once more, and tighten my arms around her, reluctant to let go.

"Come," I encourage, releasing her and sitting up.

She gives an indignant mumble but sits up too,

stretching her arms above her head. When she stands, I am momentarily distracted my all the pale golden skin on display, my cock stirs and my mouth waters. *Later* I promise myself.

I stand, scraping my locs into a knot atop my head and securing them with the leather throng that fell loose last night.

"I'm all sticky," Willow complains as she wrestles her dress on.

"My apologies," I chuckle as I fasten my robe over my shoulder.

When we are both dressed, Willow rolls up the blankets and stuffs them in her bag then wanders towards the edge of the cliffs.

I follow her, unfurling my wings, stretching them out behind me and giving the feathers a rustle. I do not feel the familiar tug on my magic, instead the act is easy, effortless.

"Are we flying back?" My mate asks as I step up behind her.

"Of course," I reply, scooping her up in my arms.

She gives a squeal of delight before flinging her arms around my neck. As I step closer to the edge of the cliff, she kisses my cheek affectionately then closes her eyes, lowering her head to rest her brow on my collarbone.

"I could get used to you carrying and flying me everywhere, but I want to learn. Will you teach me?"

I imagine soaring above the bay with my mate, dancing with her in the clouds, racing her, both of us breathless and free.

"It would be my pleasure," I tell her as I launch us into the clear blue sky overhead.

Truly I am the most blessed of fae.

Chapter 28

Willow

I keep my eyes closed until I feel Vias land, and he gently sets me on my feet. When I open them, we are on my balcony. With a hand between my shoulder blades, he leads me into the room. It feels strange now, knowing that I have accepted this place as my home.

"I'll leave you to freshen up," Vias says, turning to face me. "Later we can collect your things and find places for them in my chambers."

"Your chambers?"

He steps closer to me, eyes smouldering, and my knees feel weak. My breath hitches when he takes my chin between his thumb and index finger, leaning down to kiss me. It is warm and gentle, full of affection.

"Forgive me, *our* chambers. You are my High Lady now, what is mine, is yours."

My tummy flutters at the resonant rumble of his voice and all I can do is smile up at him.

"I'll return soon, then we can make our first appearance together, to bid our friends farewell."

"Alright," I agree, excitement and a little apprehension thrumming through me.

"Until then." Vias kisses me again, his lips hot and

possessive, full of promise.

Heat gathers and pools between my legs and my heart stutters. I suck in a breath and squeeze my thighs together as I watch my mate leave the room.

My mate.

I expected to feel uneasy after accepting the bond, frightened by the finality of it. But I don't. Seki was right; as soon as I made my decision it felt like everything fell into place. My worries dissolved and were replaced with a feeling of rightness, of belonging. I was meant to come through that portal, just as I was meant to meet Vias. My mate.

Grinning like a fool I make my way to the bathroom. I cringe at my reflection, though I can't regret how I came to look so dishevelled. After dragging my brush through my hair to rid it of knots I tip my head upside down and scuff my fingers along the roots to fluff my hair up a little. I don't have time to wash it.

I fill the basin with hot water and strip off, frantically cleaning myself. Of course, I would much prefer a nice long soak in the tub, as I'm still wonderfully achy from last night…and this morning, but I don't know how long I have, so hot water and a cloth will have to do.

Once I'm squeaky clean I make my way back into my room and consider what to wear. The dress I wore yesterday and this morning could probably use a wash. I doubt my patchwork skirt and a vest top will be suitable… that only leaves a creamy dress I have. It's floor length with capped sleeves and some delicate silver beading around the waist. I slip it over my head and tighten the fastenings.

I'm debating whether or not I can get away with going barefoot, or at least wearing my flip flops when there is a knock at my door. Before I have a chance to open it, Vias enters, and I let out an audible sigh at the sight of him.

Was I concerned that once I accepted the bond, I would feel nothing for this male? Ha! He's changed into a navy-blue toga that has gold trim along the edges and has once again donned his sun medallion and circlet. His wings are on display proudly behind him, shimmering with hints of gold. He looks magnificent. I grin, knowing that having his wings on display no longer *costs* him his magic, that it is now infinite. Though I would never have stayed simply to fulfil it, forsaking my own happiness, it is certainly a pleasant bonus.

I can't help myself; I race across the room and fling my arms around him and crush my mouth to his. He lets out a surprised huff, then kisses me back, matching my passion.

When he pulls away, he is grinning ear to ear. "You know, its bad form to attend a formal event with a tented skirt."

"Sorry," I giggle, but I'm not really.

"I have something for you," he informs me, handing me a shallow square box the size of a dinner plate.

I work the filigree clasp then lift the lid and gasp. Inside, resting on a silky padded cushion is a delicate circlet. It's similar to Vias'; embossed with the court emblem, but it's thinner and made of silver.

"It's beautiful," I exclaim.

"It was my mother's."

My gaze darts up to him. I expect to see sadness in his eyes, but instead I find only pride. "May I?" he asks.

I nod and he takes the box from my hands, removing the circlet and placing the box on a nearby table. With the utmost care and concentration, he sets the delicate silver band across my brow, arranging my hair around it.

"Beautiful," he grins, brushing the back of his fingers against my cheek. "Shall we?"

He takes my hand and leads me from the room without waiting for my response. His fingers are warm entwined with mine and I follow him, mesmerised by the gorgeous man beside me.

Hand in hand we walk leisurely down the hall, and I behold it anew now that it's my home. This palace, with its bright white marble corridors, golden details and breath-taking views of the bay is my *home.* I do a little happy dance on the inside as Vias leads me down the stairs to the foyer. At the far end of the spacious room is a wide archway that leads out into the courtyard where the others await our arrival. It suddenly dawns on me that I don't have a clue what I'm doing.

"Wait," I whisper, halting and tugging on Vias' hand. He turns and looks at me with a concerned frown.

"What is it?"

"I… I don't know what I'm doing. You said I'm High Lady now, but I don't know how to be one. I don't have to give a speech, or anything do I?"

My mate chuckles and takes a step closer, cupping my cheek with his palm.

"Willow, for today I only wish you to accompany me. If in the future you wish to have more involvement at court, then we can discuss which responsibilities and duties you wish to undertake. But you will never be made to do anything you don't want to."

"Okay."

I breathe a sigh of relief as Vias leans in and gives me a gentle kiss, his thumb caressing my cheek.

"Ready?" He asks as he pulls away.

"Ready," I confirm with a smile, feeling reassured by my mate's words.

Vias gives my hand an affectionate squeeze, then leads us across the foyer and out into the courtyard.

Everyone has gathered, ready to depart. Horses have been saddled, carts have been laden with supplies and court guards stand to attention in their polished armour. I do not envy them in this heat.

All eyes turn to us as we descend the last few marble steps. The gravel crunches underfoot and I'm glad I wore my flip flops. My heart thumps in my chest as everyone assesses what they're seeing; the silver circlet on my head, my hand entwined with the High Lords. I look sideways at the male beside me, and he glances back at me with a beaming smile of both pride and adoration.

Seki is the first to approach. "You made your decision I see."

"Yeah," I grin.

"I'm pleased for you. Both of you."

"Thanks. You were right, as soon as I made the decision to stay everything just kind of… fell into place." She smiles at me knowingly.

Vias squeezes my hand again then releases it to head over to the High Lord of Autumn. They clasp each other's forearm, then clap each other on the shoulder before launching into a conversation about their mates.

"Does this mean you're not coming with us?" Edith asks as she approaches next, Charlotte at her side.

"I'm afraid not."

Char's bottom lip trembles and she flings her arms around me. I give her a big hug before she pulls away, her eyes watery.

"I'd stay but…this heat is killing me. Both of us!" She glances at Edith who nods.

"I guess this means my brother will finally stop moping about!" K exclaims as he joins us.

"I hope so," I reply.

"You look gorgeous by the way. High Lady suits you."

I feel my cheeks blush and I laugh awkwardly as I dip my gaze. All this attention is weird, but I suppose I'll have to get used to it. When I look back up at him, I realise he is wearing travel attire.

"Wait, you're leaving too?"

The grin he gives me is all boyish charm. "I am indeed! Where my mate goes, I follow."

"Mate?!"

K glances over his shoulder and I follow his gaze as it lands on two humans stood looking uncomfortable by their horses. Amber and Riley.

"Oh! I nearly forgot. Here." K hands me a small box, and when I open it, I find it full of tiny identical sticks.

"Matches! To help with your herbs." He gives me a cheeky wink then before I can thank him, he darts across the courtyard towards Amber and Riley. I feel a little stab of regret that I didn't get to spend more with them at the bonfire last night. I wonder why they are travelling to Spring Court. Then it dawns on me that *everyone* is leaving.

"Oh man, if K is leaving too, who am I going to hang out with when V—my mate is doing High Lord things?"

Edith and Charlotte exchange conspiratorial looks. "Well, Mollie is staying," the latter informs me.

"She is?"

"Yep, she made some excuse about it being because she wants to 'remain close to Autumn Court ready for when they send us back,' but I saw her sneak off with the High Lord's twin at the bonfire last night!"

"No!" I gasp, surely not. They *hate* each other.

Char just shrugs with a mischievous expression on her face.

Mollie isn't my favourite person in the world, but it will be nice to have another human around… well, I guess I'm not human anymore, but still. I seek the tiny blonde out in the crowd and find her near the back of the group talking heatedly with Sascha. My mate's twin is nowhere to be seen.

"Time to go, my sweet mate," the High Lord of Autumn announces as he joins us. Coming up behind

Seki he rests his hands on her arms and plants a kiss on her shoulder. She preens under his affection.

"You ready?" She asks the others.

When they nod, she walks away with her mate. Char and Edith linger, waiting until we are alone, then both of them squeeze me into another hug, a Willow sandwich. I giggle and hug them both back.

"I'm gunna miss you," I whine, and they both mumble their responses into my shoulders.

I've become very attached to these two in our time here so far, and I'm sad to see them go. But I know my place is here with Vias. There would be nothing stopping me from visiting them either, maybe I could even fly over to Spring Court. I smile at the thought.

The supplies are checked one final time, then everyone saddles up and forms a neat line facing the huge archway that leads out of the courtyard. Vias comes up beside me and wraps his arm around my shoulders pulling me close. I wind my arm around his waist, resting my head against him, earning myself a kiss on the top of my head, and watch my friends leave.

It's a strange feeling, being left behind by the others, Mollie excluded of course, but at the same time feeling more complete and happier than I ever have before. I wonder how Mollie is feeling about all this and consider going to speak to her, offer comfort maybe, but I see she has already disappeared. Later then, perhaps.

"Right then, my High Lady, shall I show you to your chambers?"

"I thought they were *our* chambers," I giggle.

"Forgive me, I was distracted," he tells me, nuzzling into my neck.

How easy it has become between us in such a short amount of time.

Vias leads the way back through the palace, my hand firmly held in his, to a part of the south wing I had not yet explored. He pushes open one of two doors but then steps aside so I can enter first.

My jaw hits the floor.

The room I have entered is more like a foyer, open and airy, with lush rugs dotted along the floor, velvety chaises and dozens of potted plants adding dashes of vibrant green. My mate leads me right, to two doors a few feet apart. I open the first to reveal a closet. A closet!

"I will see to it that you have some clothes made with the court sigil, and anything else you need," my mate tells me, but I am stunned into silence.

I open the second door to reveal a bathroom, but it's not like any bathroom I have seen before, except maybe on those TV shows where they give tours of famous people's homes. In the center is a bath—a pool really—sunk into the floor, and beyond it is a shower faucet. All the fixtures are gold, and there are patches of blue mosaic everywhere and one corner boasts a stack of the plushest looking towels I have ever seen.

Vias leads me back across the foyer to the other side where double doors await. He pushes them open to reveal the bedroom. Oh my God. Against the back wall is a huge bed, big enough for five people, and dotted around the room are more plants: mini palm trees in pots and brightly coloured flowers. To the right translucent golden gossamer curtains flutter in the breeze, leading out to a balcony that looks out over the court and I can already see the crystalline water in the bay.

"This… this is insane," I breathe. "This is really mine? Ours?"

"It is," my mate reassures me from the doorway.

I can't help but squeal with glee. This is fancier than even my wildest dreams. In a moment of sheer excitement, I dart across the room and fling myself onto the bed, landing on my back. Vias crosses the room and joins me, laying to one side then sliding his arm around my waist and pulling me close.

"You approve then?"

"It'll do," I tease.

He chuckles then dips his head to kiss me. I lean into him, a soft moan of appreciation on my lips. After a moment he pulls away, gazing down at me with nothing short of adoration and brushes a rouge curl away from my face.

"So, where do you think you will travel to first?" He asks, a hint of sadness in his voice.

I cup his cheek as I search my feelings on the matter before answering. "Nowhere," I tell him, caressing the cool brown skin beneath my thumb. "I don't feel the tug of wanderlust yet."

"No?" He smiles.

"No," I confirm.

"Will you tell me when you do?"

"Of course. But right now, I am exactly where I want to be."

It's the truth. I have never felt more… grounded. As if I have truly found my place. My home. I know I am free to explore as much as my heart desires, but Summer Court and Vias, will forever be my true home. The thought is comforting and makes me glow with happiness.

I lean forward and brush my lips against his. When his mouth parts on a groan I slide my tongue along his bottom lip, before dipping inside seeking his. The kiss turns heated, more passionate and full of promise, until Vias breaks away.

"Before I tear this dress off you and worship your body for as long as you'll let me my sweet mate, there is one last thing I wish to show you."

"What's that?" I ask, still a little dazed from our kiss.

"Ethea."

"Ethea?"

"Yes," he chuckles, rising from the bed and holding out his hand. I take it and he pulls me up to stand in front of him.

"I want to fly with you, up above our court and show you all that this world has to offer you. But you must promise me something."

"What?"

"That you'll keep your eyes *open*."

"Alright," I giggle.

A squeal escapes me as he scoops me up in his arms, his wings already rusting eagerly behind him. I wind my arms around his muscular neck, trusting him completely. My gorgeous, thoughtful mate.

"Eyes open," he reminds me.

I nod excitedly as he hauls me against his chest, holding me tightly. Anticipation thrums through me as he carries me to the balcony. Overhead the sky is a clear perfect blue, not a cloud to be seen.

"Ready?"

"Ready," I breathe, my heart in my throat.

Vias kisses my cheek, his wings beating behind him, then with an adoring grin he surges into the sky, and we take flight.

Want more Willow and Vias?
Check out my Patreon for a bonus Honeymoon scene, and more.
https://www.patreon.com/LunaDaye

Acknowledgements

I was not expecting to tell this story. But once the idea came to me, it flew out onto the page. After sharing the story with my incredible Alphas, they encouraged me to let it lose on the world. So here we are!

As always, thank you to my amazing fiancée, Becks. Without you, I would never have had the confidence to follow my dreams. Thank you for listening and always being there for me. I am eternally grateful for all your love and support.

To my alphas; Ally, Gyselle, and Jenni. I couldn't have done it without you. Thank you for being there for me when I got stuck, and for letting me ramble about all the ideas swirling in my head. Thank you for cheering me on and encouraging me.

Thank you to my betas: Adele, and Sarah. Your feedback was invaluable

To my author friends. Special shout out to Aelina and Jordan. Thank you for encouraging me and letting me pick your brains when I got stuck!

To my Tiktok friends. Special shout out to Lizz. Thank you for all your support and encouragement.

To Sarah de Lang, from Moonrosesxart. My awesome cover designer. Thank you for bringing my ideas to life.

To my family and friends. Thank you all, so much, for believing in me, and supporting me.

To the writers who came before me. There are too many of you to list. But thank you to every author who has put their story out there. You fill my life with magic, adventure, love (and sometime pain!) You have inspired and encouraged me to create stories of my own.

Lastly to my readers. Thank you for taking a chance on an indie author, for your support, and beautiful words of praise.

With all my heart, *thank you.*

If you have enjoyed Fae's Flight, please consider leaving a review, or telling a friend.

ABOUT THE AUTHOR

Luna lives in North Devon, UK and has been writing stories for as long as she can remember. When Luna isn't writing, curled up with a good book or making TikTok videos, she can usually be found playing video games with her fiancée Becks, walking her pug Dexter, or working on one of her many craft projects.

Don't miss out on new releases, sign up to my newsletter!
Lunadaye.com

Printed in Great Britain
by Amazon

27255817R00118